THE ARRANGED MARRIAGE

MONICA ARYA

To the kindest, most hardworking and compassionate humans I know-my parents. Mom and Pop, I love you both and am grateful for the life you built from scratch for us, but also the choice you gave us to build our own lives, too.

To those that have always been told to live their life a certain way. I hope that you find the courage and strength to remember rules are meant to be broken and you deserve to live the life you've always dreamt of. This is our now.

AUTHOR'S NOTE

Dear reader,

I am so honored you chose my book to spend time with. As with all of my thriller novels this book contains some trigger warnings. I hope that you will protect your peace and check those out on my website www.monicaarya.com. It isn't as dark as some of my other thrillers such as The Favorite Girl and The Next Mrs. Wimberly but there are some—there's cannibalism so I think that warrants a heads-up.

This is not the sequel to The Favorite Girl. The Caged Girl is the sequel. This is a standalone paranormal thriller to celebrate my love for scary movies and ghost stories. I wanted to have some wicked fun and write a book based on a folklore I grew up being scared of.

My mom actually did have an arranged marriage

so this book was one she has always wanted me to write with my own unhinged spin.

If you don't like ghosts and deranged spirits then my other thrillers do not have that but this one does. If you do like them, I hope you enjoy meeting this one.

Sending my good vibes always,

Monica Arya

AUTHOR'S SECOND NOTE

If you've ever heard a strange creaking in your house, had your feet hang off of the bed and feel something brush against them, maybe you've seen a light flicker or felt a cold gust of air…it was probably a ghost. I know you convinced yourself otherwise but…

Oh no.

Don't look now. Don't look over your shoulder…

She's right there.

Dakini (noun) - In ancient literature and many folklore stories, dakinis are tormented spirits. A Dakini emerges from a dead woman and can craft herself into any form and any illusion in order to seek revenge on a man that has hurt her.

PROLOGUE

A WARM, humid gust of wind causes the rows of wheat to sway as we look into the well. My older sister, Amara, purses her lips before releasing them and howling into it to create a silly echo. Laughter erupts from the depths of my stomach as I clutch it from the cramps that follow.

"Amara didi!" I wince as she tethers the edge and wiggles her foot in. 'Didi' translates to big sister in Hindi.

"Don't be frightened, Gia." A coy smile emerges on her face as she repeats the irresponsible action. We are playing at an old well on our family's farm as the sun sinks into the endless golden wheat.

Closing my eyes, a wave of nausea floods over my body as a feeling of doom washes over me. Amara's giggles don't soothe the anxiety I feel. My skin no longer feels warm as my hands grow frigid, even though it has to be at least ninety-degrees with suffocating humidity gripping into my lungs. I look at my sister as she dangles her foot into the well, when suddenly, stillness overtakes my body.

"You're going to die." I'm shocked at the words that trickle out of my mouth in a hushed, regretful whisper. I feel a pit in my stomach, knowing my sister *is* going to die. We all will, but she… she is going to die earlier. A vision flashes across my eyes as I picture her laying lifeless and pale.

"Amara didi, fall back!" I force myself to shout, though the words seem to pour out of my lips that aren't moving at the same speed as the words.

Amara tilts her head and looks down into the well. Her foot slips slightly, and she shoots her arms out to regain her balance.

"Didi!" I scream, but just as her body folds over, a small, yellow butterfly flutters out and Amara tumbles backward onto the deep, red clay dirt. The butterfly dances around me slowly as my mind lags, and I'm watching it in awe.

A cold breeze circles around me as I collapse next to Amara, and the butterfly leaves us in disbelief.

"That butterfly saved your life," I breathe out as I rest my body weight on my dirtied palms.

Amara's chest rises and falls rapidly as she slowly

turns her head to me. Tears flood her beautiful caramel-brown eyes as moisture catches in her thick lashes I'd always been envious of.

"No, Gia… you did. You're my little butterfly." She leans closer and plants a kiss on my cheek as tears escape my eyes.

I don't tell my sister, but as she wraps her arms around me, I clench my eyes shut and see it again.

A haunting image and nauseating sensation over-takes any clarity I'm fighting to gain back. I see my sister laying somewhere dark and dirty that I don't recognize. She's lifeless with bruises. Blood, and grime are clinging to her usually glowing, deep-brown skin.

She can't be older than twenty-four, and she's dead. Opening my eyes, I look at her and she whispers, "I know. I see it, too. I'm worried, my little butterfly. I'm so scared of what's going to happen to me. I just want to love and live."

Padding her fingertips across my cheek, she forces out a pain-filled grin, which does nothing for the tight-ness encasing my heart as I stare back at her. I don't want my sister to die a painful death, but I know she will.

MY HEART POUNDED against my chest as I clutched my arms around myself in a protective hug. "No, Papa! I'm begging you, please don't make me do this!" I screeched as we sat together on a worn bench and looked out at the mostly dead farm.

His arm snaked around me as he watched the sun set over the endless rows of what should have been hearty wheat.

"Beta," the loving word he always called me— something many Indian parents called their children, but oddly enough, it translated to 'son'.

"No…" I fought back the tears as the scorching summer sun burned my olive skin. The sky looked like sherbet with not a tree in sight, swirls of deep orange and soft pinks blurring together.

"I'm not asking you, Gia; I'm telling you. Raj gave

me a loan to save the farm. We would have lost it completely, along with the house, had he not shown such generosity. He is a kind man and is simply shattered. He loved your sister, and within a few short years, he became widowed."

Shaking my head, I cupped my face as my heart raced and I looked out into the field. It didn't look saved. But I suppose something can look like it's thriving when all it's really doing is surviving.

"How can I marry Amara's husband?" The words tasted bitter on my tongue as I said them. "Papa… she *died* there." I looked at my father, who wouldn't shift his eyes to me. I hated how he kept them forward as the lines deepened around them, melting into his deep brown skin that had been aged faster with the unforgiving sun he'd spent hours upon hours under.

"He is a respectable man, Gia. Who is going to agree to marry a widower carrying the burden of his loss? We've ruined his life, and this is the only way we can balance the scales. We have to maintain good karma." My father slowly turned toward me as his almond-shaped eyes filled with tears.

"If you don't agree to marry him, we will lose everything, and no one will marry you, anyway. Who will marry the girl of a family with one dead daughter and no money?"

My body tensed at the reality of what he was

saying. "We never got to talk to Amara while she was in America. She just wrote the occasional letter that didn't even sound like her. What if I never get to see you or talk to you, Papa?" I swallowed the lump in my throat, thinking of how my sweet, soft-spoken sister hardly called us while she was abroad for years. She said Raj's mother didn't like her to talk on the phone, so instead, she needed to write letters—letters they would read before mailing over. None of this was a red flag to my parents. They reassured us both, saying this was a common practice, even amongst their friends. They were more concerned with basking in how everyone respected them so much more because their daughter was married to a wealthy man from America.

Closing my eyes, I pictured my sister in her stunning red and golden bridal outfit, spinning around as laughter echoed around her. I envied that she'd get to live in America, but I didn't envy that she was getting married. No, she was marrying a stranger; how could I ever envy that? Instead, it provided as a reminder that I, too, would one day be forced to marry a man I'd never get to know before becoming his property. But Amara was nothing like me.

Tears streamed down my cheeks, and then I felt my father's jagged fingers brush them away. Little did he realize he'd never be able to heal the shattered heart inside my body that I had always felt as a woman, especially in a small village in India. My sister had a chance at a lifetime of dreams and freedom. She had a chance, but instead, she left our home in a wedding dress and came back home in an urn.

Was that going to be my fate, too? But what choice did I have? I couldn't stay here, where my parents would resent me as they spiraled into further distress. I didn't have a choice, but I desperately wanted one.

"Gia…say yes."

Opening my eyes, I looked back at him, and although the sticky humidity clung to the nape of my neck, I trembled with the chills that shook my body. I felt febrile as my body physically reacted to what was now conspiring in front of me.

"What if I say no?" I whispered, keeping my eyes low as I inhaled the scent of dirt, warmth, and fear.

"That's why I didn't give you an option."

"I suppose I should have known from the minute I was born a girl that I'd never have options." I forced myself to say before my father laced his calloused hand with mine.

Tugging something out of his pocket, he opened my other hand and gently laid a beautiful necklace with a butterfly pendant.

"Papa, what is this?" I questioned as I traced my fingers against the stunning necklace.

"Amara wanted you to have this before she left for

America. I suppose I forgot, amongst all the wedding festivities and the struggles of the farm. I don't know what it means, but I'm sure you do."

Nodding, I bit back the wave of emotion that crashed through me. Ever since the incident at the well, I always credited the butterfly for saving Amara. However, she never did. She said I was her butterfly. I was her light. I didn't find it coincidental that I was receiving this necklace now. It's as if Amara knew all along that I'd need it in my greatest time of darkness. I'd need to remember to shine. But I didn't want to. I didn't want to shine for a man I didn't want to marry. Or a man that was in love with my older sister.

"She'd want you to be happy, and so do we." Papa tipped my head to him and kissed the top. The small gesture hurt me more than helped me because physical affection was rare in our family, and now, with my father was showing it to me, I only wanted to cling tighter.

We sat there until the sun vanished into the land that would never be home for me again. I soaked it all in before the darkness came, because something told me this would be the last time I'd ever see the only place I'd ever known. I knew the only way I'd come back home wasn't while living and breathing.

No, I'd probably be in an urn, too.

CHAPTER
TWO

IN HINDI, the national language of India, there is no word for divorce. It's as if there's this suffocating precedent set that there is no way out of the legal and religious sanctity of marriage. The worst part is that the man you're supposed to spend your life with is often times a complete stranger. I always knew there wasn't an option for me to fall in love and marry someone my parents didn't choose for me. I knew there was no point of getting to know the handsome guy that smiled at me. I knew I'd end up wasting my time, breaking my own heart and resenting my parents even more.

But now, here I stand, wearing my sister's wedding lengha. The traditional, beautiful, and bright red beaded skirt with a short blouse and stunning scarf pinned into my hair. We didn't have the money to purchase a new bridal dress for me, nor did we have the money for the stunning jewelry. My mother clasped the heavy necklace around my neck while my cousin carefully slid the bangles around my wrists. She made me promise to give them back to her since it was her original wedding set. The nose ring was tugging uncomfortably as they clipped it in, even though my piercing had closed, my mother jammed the metal through to open it back up without second thought. The intricate henna covered my hands in a deep burgundy as I stood there, outwardly dressed as a bride, but inside I felt like I was going to my own funeral.

The house wasn't full of laughter, color, and fragrance as it was when Amara got married. No, it was mostly quiet and somber. My parents didn't invite anyone to celebrate my wedding day; instead, just a few close family members pushed their way in while casting their judgment, just to watch the spectacle my life had now become.

Hushed whispers echoed around as aunties, uncles, and cousins gossiped. I fought back the tears and was faced away from the mirror. I couldn't see myself as a bride, not yet. I didn't necessarily dream of my wedding day the way most girls did—I really never wanted to get married. I wanted to have a sexual relationship with a man, I just didn't care to nurture the ego of one.

I knew most of the men my parents would have potentially tried to arrange a marriage with would have been childish boys, so coddled by their parents that I wouldn't be a wife, but rather a mother.

Now, here I was, a twenty-five-year-old virgin bride about to marry her dead sister's thirty-six-year-old husband.

"My beautiful Gia." My mother sniffled as she carefully brushed her hand under my chin. My cousin had plastered my face with heavy makeup, three shades too light, that felt smothering on my usually bare skin. Lighter skin was superior to many in our culture, even though I loved the melanin that crafted the perfect deep caramel skin I was grateful for.

"Make me proud." Stupidly, I had hoped she'd say another three words. "I love you," or maybe "Don't marry him". But instead, she said a simple statement that told me I had no way out. I was expected to be subservient—my one and only job in life. Make my parents proud, then make my husband and in-laws proud. The only person I was failing was myself.

The priest chanted in Sanskrit as my youngest cousin tied our dupattas, the long scarves from both of our outfits, together. I was then forced to follow Raj around the blazing fire as holy verses were sung, promising our seven lives together.

Didn't he promise my sister this only a few years ago? How could we spend seven lives together if he had already promised Amara?

His eyes lit up when he saw me walking down the aisle, but he dropped them down just as quickly. His mother wasn't able to attend, nor did any of his family members make the trip. Even when he married Amara, he had only brought a few cousins with him, explaining the international travel would be too daunting on his aging, disabled mother.

Once we stopped walking around the fire, we stood in front of each other and exchanged the small, thin golden rings.

"Here," he pulled out a large diamond engagement ring and my eyes widened in shock. I didn't expect this. Amara wasn't even given a diamond, just a simple band—and I hoped it wasn't the one that was now on my finger.

Raj lifted my hand into his and slid the massive diamond onto my finger. He was a physician. What more could anyone want in a husband? What was wrong with me for being so reluctant?

"I will give you anything you want, just give me a son." He brushed his hand against my cheek, and my entire body tensed. But it wasn't in a stressful way, it was in a way that made me want him to touch me more.

Nodding slowly, I bit down on my bottom lip, ashamed that I was having these emotions for a man I didn't even know, and worst of all, Amara's husband.

We grew up with an overpowering repression on anything sexual that this is what I had come down to.

But now he wasn't my dead sister's husband; he was mine, and I was his.

I looked out at the chairs that were filled with a few family members and froze. My mother was holding the blue vase in her hands, clutching it tightly while crying.

The thick, fake eyelashes made it challenging to see clearly, but I knew she wasn't crying because she was going to miss me or because she was happy for me. No, she was crying because I knew she wished I was the daughter in that jar, not her precious Amara.

Amara was the more beautiful daughter, the more obedient one, and most of all, the one who always made me look bad because she set the bar so ridiculously high.

Well, look where that got you, sister, I thought to myself, knowing it was repulsive to even think that way.

Glancing back at Raj, I decided I was ready to leave this life. I was ready to leave this life of rules and ridiculous societal expectations. I was ready for America—the land of the free and where dreams come true.

I just didn't realize the only thing that would come true would be my nightmares.

WE WEREN'T GOING to have a beautiful reception the way Raj and Amara did. Instead, we simply sat at the plastic folding table and ate dinner with my family. A child's birthday party would have been more elaborate than this. Part of me was envious about how Raj paid for a giant, beautiful wedding for Amara. It was gorgeous, with music, florals, mouth-watering food, and brightly colored outfits. He knew my father couldn't afford it, which only made my family double-down at his feet even more.

I ate a few bites before the nerves of what was to come rippled through me as I watched Raj and my father have a serious conversation. My mother kept away from me, just rushing around, pretending every-thing was fine with the family who had come to be here. I sat there silently like the good wife I was expected to be.

The stitching of my heavy gown pricked at my skin, and I ran my fingers against the detailed beading my mother had embroidered into the silky, red fabric for Amara.

She didn't even offer to stitch me a simple outfit. We didn't even have the money to fill one suitcase for me to take to America. I was embarrassed by the faded blouses and slacks my mother—who huffed with irritation about losing one of her suitcases—crammed into a small bag for me to take. But now my life would change. I would be married to an American doctor, and I wouldn't have to live like this anymore.

Raj leaned toward me and whispered into my ear, "Shall we go to our room?" The warmth of his breath intertwined with the spices of the meal in front of him made my chest tighten.

"Yes." I looked down at my full plate and stood with him. Perhaps my resentment toward my family fueled my urge to be with him. We didn't even do the ceremonial farewell, but my mother waved me away without a second thought. I knew she didn't care about upholding the traditions for me. In one week, my mother was given an urn with her daughter's ashes and married the other to the same man. I was positive my mother's mind was frail and she'd internalize every ounce of emotion as she was raised to do.

I was embarrassed to even look at my father or male relatives. Sex was such a taboo topic, and everyone knew where we were going and what we would be doing. Although the Kama Sutra was created in India, there was no talk about anything related to sex. Sex was to create a family; sex was to pleasure men.

I had never been kissed, or touched, or had even seen a naked man's body. I was sheltered for twenty-five years of my life, and here we were, driving to the nearby hotel and my head felt fuzzy as we walked in.

The heavy scarlet skirt trailed behind me as my jewelry jingled and the hotel staff congratulated us. This was the first time I was in a hotel, and I was here with a stranger. My heart sank as I realized the magnitude of it all.

I was in a hotel with a stranger. I was about to sleep with a stranger. But that stranger was also my husband.

My stomach flipped as he laced his fingers with mine, and I followed behind him through the door. The room was enormous, and the scent of fresh florals floated in the air. The king-sized bed was covered in gorgeous shades of red, pink, and blush rose petals.

It was actually romantic.

I stood there like a statue, not knowing what I was

supposed to do. No one told me or explained what I should be doing. I knew the basic idea of sex and kissing. Amara and I would sneak and look through dated magazines of American celebrities kissing, but we didn't have phones or even internet. The only time we could look things up online was at the local café hotspot and there was no way we could get away with searching about sex or love.

Raj didn't speak; instead, he cornered me into the wall and tilted my face gently. Lifting a small tube of clearly-used, red lipstick, he twisted it upward. He began tracing my lips with it while smiling.

"Now you're her." It was my sister's lipstick. My breathing hitched. He had painted my lips with my dead sister's lipstick on our wedding night. His head tilted slightly as a small smirk grew on his face.

"Do you want to know the one thing dead and living women have in common?" He whispered as the tip of his nose brushed against mine.

Swallowing the lump in my throat, my eyes grew glossy as I stifled the sob choking me.

"Both dead and living women look beautiful with lipstick on." Raj winked at me before wrapping his hands around my throat and tugging me in.

His lips crashed into mine so quickly that I let out a small gasp against his mouth. It went from a sweet kiss to a more aggressive, needy kiss. He pushed his tongue into my mouth.

I didn't understand; my emotions were scattered. I felt numb by his terrifying words but everything blurred. He continued shoving his tongue against mine and I felt like I was going to gag. My mind was racing with everything I should do, but I stood there, pinned against the wall as he was licking and kissing me without stopping once. His hands were around my waist where my blouse didn't meet my skirt, and the way his fingers padded against my bare skin had my thighs clenching together tightly.

Before I knew it, my outfit was piled onto the floor, and I was left standing there in nothing but my jewelry. Raj was still fully dressed, and the way his eyes dripped down my entire body sent chills up my spine. I began to anxiously attempt to unclasp the heavy necklace, but he reached out and gripped my hand. "No, leave it on," he said in a hushed whisper. I covered my breasts with one arm and dropped my hand below.

Turning my body towards the foot of the bed, he pushed me onto the bed without hesitation. There I was, laying naked with my bangles chiming around my wrists. I looked at him for a moment before cutting my eyes away out of embarrassment.

I had no idea what I was doing. I had no idea how

to be 'sexy' or what to say. Raj undressed and then dropped down to his knees. Spreading my legs, he pressed his face in between, and that's when my eyes slammed shut and noises I didn't even recognize escaped from my lips.

Everything was a haze. He eventually crawled up to me and ran his fingers against me before shoving them into my mouth.

Gasping, he looked at me. "Taste how sweet you are, Gia," he rasped before stroking himself and gently pushing inside me. My nails dug into the sheet as I rolled my lips together tightly to suppress not the moans of pleasure, but the sounds of pain that were ripping through my body as he picked up his pace and tossed his head back, enjoying every sensation. I kept my eyes closed and realized something…

He wasn't wearing protection. Slowly opening my eyes, I looked at him while he groaned and I mumbled, "Raj… I'm not on the pill."

He stopped and smirked at me. "It doesn't matter, Amara. You need to give me a son now. You have to, Amara." He ground his teeth before telling me to turn around. My body was shaking as tears grew in my eyes. He called me by my dead sister's name… He was fantasizing about my sister on our wedding night.

"On all fours. Now," he ordered as my body grew numb and moved, trying to understand what he wanted me to do. I felt so exposed with the light above blasting on us and no blanket to hide under.

He didn't even take a moment to just talk to me, to kiss me, or let me feel comfortable. We are prohibited to have one-night stands or pre-marital sex, but this... this was okay?

I positioned myself and immediately, he jerked my hips higher from behind, digging his nails into my skin. I looked down at the white bedding and saw blood. Heat pooled in my cheeks as he continued to move inside me, and everything ached. I wanted him to stop. "Amara... yes!" he moaned over and over again.

"Please stop. I'm not Amara." I cried out in pain, but it wasn't just physical; now, it was also emotional.

He didn't stop.

He grabbed my hair in his hands, tugging it back aggressively and breathed out, "I need you, Amara. I missed you, my love."

Just like that, tears rolled down my cheeks as I stared at the headboard, knowing there was no way I would get on the airplane with this man in the morning.

He let out a loud, obnoxious, but satisfied, scream. Clenching my eyes shut, I knew he'd never let me stay behind. I could be pregnant after this. My parents would rather watch me burn to ashes than keep a tainted, married daughter in their home.

"Oh, Amara…" He sighed and laid next to me as I let my body collapse. Brushing my hair from my face, he studied me before swiping his thumb under my tear-stained eye.

A small smile grew across his face as he shoved his thumb into his mouth. "Even your pain is delicious, just like hers." Letting out a laugh, he turned away as my blood went cold. I couldn't believe I was this man's wife.

But now I also knew he enjoyed relishing in her pain. And now, he'd do the same to me.

I had to run away.

I LAID next to him on our wedding night, watching him breathe and snore obnoxiously. His lips twitched as his eyelashes fluttered while lost in another world. I kept my eyes on his nostrils, thinking of how much weight I'd need to put on the pillow so I could suffocate him. I couldn't believe I was stressing about how I'd pleasure my new husband for the first half of the night, and now, a mere two hours later, I was thinking of how I could kill him without a trace.

I knew, deep down, I wouldn't be able to do it. If I murdered a fancy doctor from America—who was doing my family a favor by saving our farm and also marrying me—I'd be asking for a death sentence, for not just myself but for my parents. They didn't deserve that. But I didn't deserve this, either.

My mind was spinning just like the ceiling fan that

was cutting through the air, providing little comfort on an otherwise sweltering night. Glancing over to the window, there wasn't even a sliver of sunlight. I slowly crept out of the plush bed and tiptoed to my duffle bag, but it wasn't easy to do without my heart rate skyrocketing as my bangles and jewelry chimed with every step in the completely silent hotel room. Freezing mid-step, I held my breath as Raj spoke in his sleep.

"Amara, come back to bed," he rasped with sleep intertwined within his deep voice.

My breathing was erratic as I froze in place. "I need to use the washroom," I whispered as he sighed and fell back into his pillow.

Reaching the duffle bag, I gently pulled the zipper, but it was too loud. The rusted metal was caught, and I'd need tug it hard to open it. My mom had to send me off with her oldest bag since she knew she wouldn't get it back. Clenching my teeth together, frustration crept inside me, but I knew I couldn't waste my energy on those emotions right now.

My knees felt weak as I tried again, and luckily, the air conditioning finally cut on. The sound was a welcome form of relief as I quickly opened my bag, grabbed my clothes, and threw on a simple blouse and starched, scratchy pants. Peering over my shoulder, I sucked in a breath of air and walked over to Raj's wallet that was laid out on the dresser.

He didn't have much cash inside, and there was no way I could get away with swiping a card without being detected. I knew this was a terrible idea, but I had to leave. I would figure it out; I'd have to. I grabbed the small wad of cash and tucked it into my bag, then threw it over my shoulder. Now all I had to do was make it to the train station.

I didn't pick up my feet with each step; instead, I dragged them against the cool marble so my heel wouldn't slap against the floor and echo. Unlocking the small latch, I opened the creaking door and the hallway light poured in.

"Shit." I slid out quickly and planted one palm against the metal and slowly closed the door. Looking both ways down the empty, never-ending hallway, I ran as fast as I could toward the stairwell. I had to be gone before the sun came up and the whole village went looking for me. The hotel was right on the outskirts but the only train station I was familiar with was back towards our village. I was bound to run into someone.

My stomach rumbled. There wouldn't be food on the train, and who knew how long it would take to wherever I eventually decided was safe enough. Bombay wouldn't be a good idea, considering my only friend lived there and my parents would call her. I contemplated my limited options, hating how trapped I was.

The leftover makeup on my face felt like paint with the sticky humidity. I tugged the zipper of my jacket up higher to cover the gold necklaces around my neck. I knew I'd have to sell this jewelry once I arrived at my destination for money, but I also knew someone on the train would attack me if they saw me donning it. Sinking onto a small bench, I made sure to look around before sliding off my bangles, earrings, headpiece, and necklace, hiding it under a stack of clothes.

My heart sank as I saw the small worn velvet case holding the butterfly necklace Papa had given me from my sister. "Sorry, Papa. I can't soar here or there." Wrapping it around my neck, I brushed my fingers against the gold. Blinking away the tears that I knew were brewing, I stood back up and dragged my feet against the dirt roads before finally finding a food stall. Fresh fruit, chai, and dosas—a thin spicy crepe—were being made.

"One dosa, chai, and a banana," I said in Hindi to the thin, tired man behind the stall. He lifted his eyes, and I stumbled back. One was stitched closed, with pus oozing from it, and the other was streaked red. His one eye dropped to my hands that were covered in deep burgundy bridal henna as the small streetlight beamed down on me.

"Take the money or I'm going to the other stall." I pointed to the one down the road, trying to conceal my fear.

Nodding, he took it suspiciously as he examined my face that was still covered in bridal makeup. My heart and breathing simultaneously quickened but I had to stay calm. Men here would drag a woman back to her family if they knew she was running.

"Here." He handed me my food and the small clay cup of chai. "Pretty girls die out here." He flashed a toothless grin at me.

Grabbing the food, I jogged away from him, trying to not spill the scorching hot chai. Looking over my shoulder multiple times, I could hear him laughing in the darkness. What was I getting myself into? I had lived with my parents in a small village my entire life. Now, I was running away with no destination. Slurping the masala chai as the heat burned my throat while it went down. "Ah," I cried out.

Finally, when I knew I was far enough, I sat down watching the cows roam and the sky lose its darkness. I watched women carry tubs on top of their heads with newborn babies strapped to their chest as they headed to retrieve water from the nearest river as I ate. Their sarees were pleated neatly, even as they carried the weight of the world on their bodies.

I had to get to the train station. Raj was probably

waking up soon and then all hell would break loose. Brushing the dirt off my pants, I shoved the banana into my bag and walked quickly. But as the sun continued to rise, so did my urgency to get to the train station. I kept looking around with paranoia pooling inside me, feeling eyes on me. Pulling my hood over my hair, which was still coated in the thick, floral-scented hairspray, I scratched at my scalp. This was a disaster.

After what felt like a lifetime, I finally made it to the train station counter.

I glanced at the destinations, and sadness grew inside me. I read through the city names and realized I hadn't been to most of them. I stayed in this small, twenty-by-twenty square acre of nothing but farmland and people who either judged or gossiped about us. I went to a tiny college, which was walking distance from home, and was always deterred from making more of myself. Maybe this was the dramatic push I needed to escape this place and the never-ending hamster wheel of gender stereotypes that women were carrying and passing down through the generations.

I couldn't decide where I wanted to go when for the first time in my life, I could choose the destination.

"Just a ticket to the next departing train." I slid money against the sticky counter and the older man handed a ticket back. I didn't read it, knowing I'd obsess over the destination and fear what I'd do there. Denial was a comforting concept. Denial felt safe. I walked and sat on the bench staring at the empty tracks that had consumed so many lives.

Sometimes it would be a drunk man lying there stupidly; other times, it would be a young woman running away from her abusive in-law's house.

Standing, I walked closer to the edge and looked down. Dangling my foot off, I wondered if this was the solution I was searching for. Should I just end this cat and mouse game? Should I leave my parents with two dead daughters? Would they be able to identify my body if I was smashed into smithereens? Swallowing the little saliva in my mouth, I leaned further down, bending my body in half.

But then a strong gust of air jerked me upright as the screeching train slid down the tracks, inches away from my face. A small yellow butterfly danced around me as my heart was pounding against my chest.

Screaming, I clasped my hands over my mouth and stumbled backward as I heard my sister's voice.

"Don't do it, little butterfly."

My eyes widened. "Amara?" I rasped as I looked around wildly. I couldn't kill myself. I couldn't let my sister die in vain. Glancing once more over my shoulder, I clenched my teeth as I saw...

Was that Raj? I turned more as the train doors

opened and people bustled out. I squinted toward the bench. No, I don't think it was him. Releasing a long sigh, I smiled as I clutched the strap of my duffel bag tighter and walked onto the train. Once a few straggling people piled on, it was time to go. Making my way down to find an empty seat, my body froze.

It was Raj. Standing and staring at me from the opposite end. My jaw dropped as I shook my head and chanted 'no,' as if that would make a difference. Flinging around, I began to run back to the door, but just as I tried to escape, a strong hand gripped my jacket and pulled me straight back in.

"No! Save me, help!" I screamed out. People turned and looked at me, but no one stood up to help; no one even thought twice. Their eyes filled with pity for Raj. They were probably sympathetic with how he had to handle an unhinged, disobedient wife.

He didn't speak; instead he gripped my waist and lifted his other hand with a white handkerchief. "What…" I began, but not even a minute later, he cupped it around my nose and mouth, and everything started to blur before going black.

"You stupid woman." He rasped.

My husband had drugged me.

I OPENED my eyes slowly as a stickiness coated my lashes. Even the dim light was blinding me, but within a second of realization, I jerked upright.

Oh, no.

I was on an airplane. The soft white noise of being hundreds of thousands of feet in the air taunted me.

Turning my head slowly, there he was. *Raj.* He had headphones on and had his head tilted back against the headrest. But he knew I was watching him, because as soon as I tried to look away, his hand clutched mine.

"You're awake, sleepyhead." He smiled at me in a way that had me wishing I had laid on those train tracks.

"You drugged me," I whispered and tried to tug my hand away. "My parents… I didn't say goodbye." Hot tears stung my eyes as I looked around, completely trapped with this man thousands of miles in the air. There was nowhere to run. I had lost all my options and, as usual, I didn't even get the chance to have one.

"What did you tell them?" My voice cracked as he gripped his nails deeper into my skin, crafting territorial crescents into my flesh.

"I told them our flight had changed, and we needed to go now. They didn't mind. Now that I see how you are, I know I've done them yet another favor. Taking their deranged daughter away from them and diminishing their burden. But now, my wife, I will warn you once, and only once." Chills decorated my arms as I looked into his eyes.

Leaning in closer, the warmth of his breath grazed my face. His lips aligned to mine.

"If you ever try to run, die or disobey, I will hunt you down and slaughter you. Then, I'll send parts of your body in a matching urn, like Amara's, to your parents. After which, I will wipe any financial support I have given them and leave them to rot on the streets until the life they are living becomes unbearable and they wish to die. Something I'm more than happy to also assist with." As soon as the barbaric words poured out of his lips, he pressed them against my mouth. I was crying softly as he pushed his tongue into my mouth and swirled it around. But I was terrified. I was terrified that if I pulled away he'd do something to my parents or me. This was it; he had something to hold over my head and suffocate me with.

"You will learn to love and worship me, my beautiful wife. And in return, I will love, worship and not murder you." He smiled against my lips.

Pulling away, his eyes grew moist as he looked at me. "I loved her more than anything in the world and she loved you. I'm hoping I can love you, too… for her sake. But most of all, for our family's. You will give me a son."

Raj slid his headphones back on and closed his eyes.

The pit in my stomach deepened as I rested my head against the window, too scared to open the shade and see just how far from the ground I was with this man. I thought of my sister and how terrified she must have been on this very same flight. I wondered how long he made her suffer before he chose to take her life.

Was this the plan all along? In the few years they had been married, she did not end up pregnant. Is that why he killed her? Because she couldn't conceive? I needed answers. The only form of relief I felt was knowing his mother lived in the house we were going to live in as well. Maybe I could convince her to help me? It was better than being left alone with this monster.

But it also dawned on me that she didn't help Amara.

I closed my eyes and hoped I'd get to dream and escape from this nightmare that had become my life.

FUCK. There was blood everywhere. I stared at the small cot in front of me as she laid on her back with her frail arm dropping off the mattress. She was groaning out my name, repeating it as if she assumed I hadn't heard her. Shaking my head, I didn't care anymore. I was numb. Walking over to the sink, I turned the small knob, and the water took a moment before spraying out obnoxiously. Watching the red swirl into the cold water below was eerily satisfying to me. A year ago, I'd have gagged or screamed; I would have called out for help.

But I had changed.

And most people think change is good. As humans, we think if we change, it's to improve ourselves, to make ourselves a better version of who we are. We are expected to learn from our mistakes and grow.

But change does not always stem from growth or the desire to improve. No, sometimes, and in my case particularly, change is to protect ourselves. Selfishly.

The floors were creaking underneath my bare feet as the wind slammed against the century-old paneling of the cliffside mansion I now called home.

My unruly, thick black hair was pleated into a braid, and my thin white gown was covered in red stains. Looking down, I brushed my hand against the dried spots. Tears stung my eyes as I pulled the doors open and jerked back without letting go of the handles.

Lightning cut through the gloomy, storm-filled sky, preceded by livid thunder. Taking two steps forward, I gasped as the rain slanted and bit into my soft skin. My gown was becoming translucent as her blood began to wash out of it and stream down my legs.

I took the small black tie out, along with the tight braid, shaking my head vigorously. My hair was coated in an oil blend that Raj made me put in. He said my hair was thinning and that he deserved a wife that was always beautiful. Tossing my head back, I let the rain pellets sting my face and eyes. Two more steps forward, and I knew I was tethering on a dangerous line.

This house was falling apart, just like my life. I closed my eyes and put my hands forward. A part of the balcony railing was broken, but sometimes I'd come out here and think if I fell, then I'd escape this life I was burdened with. A life my parents forced me into because of what? Respecting our culture? Obeying them and assuming, because they gave me life, that they knew what was best for me?

My foot jammed into a piece of wood as water pooled around my toes.

"Ow," I moaned and looked down.

The waves were crashing against the enormous boulders below. I wished they'd reach higher, swallow me whole and carry me into the ocean, away from this family. Somewhere deep in the depths of the endless water so they'd have no body to burn or bury.

I stared out at the murky water.

I wondered how many people must have died in those waters? Their corpses disintegrated, perhaps mutilated by sea creatures or being slammed into the unforgiving boulders.

Chills tickled against my forearms as I swallowed the lump in my throat and parted my lips.

Watching the lightning, I whispered, "One, two, three, four..." I screamed as soon as the thunder rumbled and shook the brittle wooden balcony.

"Amara." His voice was so low, I'd have thought I imagined it, but he always knew how to find me. I couldn't hide anywhere without him detecting me.

The crumbling estate was over four-thousand

square feet, with three floors and nestled isolated from the world around it.

I didn't know this is where I'd be. My parents were shown a stunning stucco home with a white-picket fence when Raj, my so-called doting husband, came to meet Amara for the first time.

My parents were smitten. It was many parents' dream in India to see their daughter marry to an Indian-American man with a wealthy family. But Amara didn't live; she didn't survive after a couple of years. Here I was, two months in, hoping more time would fly by so I'd be killed, too. My parents told me the only way for a girl like me to get to America was to marry a good man who lived there or…be trafficked into it like Raj's cousin, Demi had been.

"My love," he called out, and I turned slowly. He was wearing scrubs. Pursing my lips, I had to bite back the impeding laughter.

"How was work today, Dr. Rao?" I mocked.

His eyes darkened as his thick, black brows lowered.

"Did you take a test today?" he asked, emotionless. My shoulders rolled forward and I instantly sucked my stomach in as if he had punched me there.

"No," I whimpered.

His jaw clenched as he shook his head angrily. "Take one, now," he hissed.

I gritted my teeth as his eyes warned me with what would happen if I didn't obey him.

Nodding, I dragged my feet through the dirty water that continued to pool on the balcony and thought of my sister going through this every month, probably wishing and praying the test would show a plus sign. I wondered how the fear must have grabbed at her every time it was a negative, and how she knew she was running out of time.

Raj said I had twelve months to get pregnant with a son, and if I didn't, something would happen to me. I decided ultimately, I would rather die than to be pregnant with his child. If it was a baby girl, what would have happened to her? I couldn't risk it. So, every time he forced his body over mine when he knew I was ovulating, I'd hold my breath and pray that nothing would happen. I'd pray not to God, but to my sister. She was the reason I was here and I hoped she'd save me the way I had once saved her. I'd live my life in sheer fear and panic until my period would come.

Except, my period was irregular—it always had been—so it made this even harder. We had been trying for two months, but not really 'we' more so, he.

"How was Mami today?" he asked as he watched me pee on the pregnancy test. He didn't trust me enough to do it unsupervised, but I had grown numb, so it didn't matter anymore, considering every single day was torture in this house.

"She did it again. And I don't blame her." I handed him the stick and began to wash my hands.

"She's debilitated from a traumatic car crash where her husband was crushed to death in the car. She doesn't want to end her life; she just needs us to care for her."

I scoffed as I looked at the man behind me in the reflection. "Sure..." I rolled my eyes and pushed past him as he laid the test down carefully.

"Amara, you know she's coming." His voice changed.

Two months of this same sentence repeated to me almost daily. But he'd never explain. I'd always ask as fear rose inside me.

"Who is coming? Raj, what is coming? And my name is Gia!" I looked at him as his face dropped and he lifted the test up.

"Fuck!" he screamed so loudly, I fell back into the closed door.

It was negative.

"We've been trying for two months. What is wrong with you? Your family is a curse to me. Even she got preg—"

He paused and composed himself.

Slanting my eyes at him, I tilted my head. "Who got

pregnant?" My heart was rapidly beating against my chest as he slammed the test into the trash bin and shoved past me to open the door.

"Was Amara pregnant?" I shouted behind him.

"Shh!" Raj flung back around and pushed me into the counter.

"She's coming." His eyes flicked wildly around us as he pressed his finger against his lips.

"Ah!" Raj's mother screamed out.

"She'll hear you!" He dropped to the ground and held his legs to his chest.

I looked around and suddenly, the air shifted, a cold, haunting breeze floating around as the door flung opened swiftly and hit me in the back. The lights flickered and I could hear Raj's mother wail from her bed.

Opening the door, I ran out to her through the dark house where the windows shook and lightning crackled again.

It wasn't a ghost; it was a fucking storm. I rolled my eyes as I made my way to her room.

The fork was on the floor tinged in her blood. Every so often she'd find a way to use a fork, or a hairbrush, or even a book to hurt herself with. We never knew how'd she get the item, considering she was completely bed-ridden, but I was absolutely certain Raj was bringing these things to her in his altered state of mind.

If it stormed, I knew I had to prepare for the worst. He regressed to a terrified child-like state and grew delusional with the wind and rain. Thunder crackled again, and the cool gusts of air blew through the windows that weren't properly sealed.

"You need to stop doing this, Mami." I looked at her with annoyance as I grabbed the towel from the faded, rough wooden floors.

I knew I should have spoken to her with more respect, but the biggest blessing of this whole nightmare was that, at least my mother-in-law could barely speak and couldn't move from the small cot she laid on. In some twisted way, her presence comforted me, knowing I wasn't alone with him here. In my new home, shadows roamed more than the light.

She'd groan out some words here and there, but nothing ever made sense. Most of the time her eyes were sealed shut, sobbing.

I left her there and went to our bedroom. Well, my bedroom since Raj and I slept separately. I suppose that was another blessing. We only shared a bed when he knew I was ovulating. I sat down on the small bed and pulled out my notebook. I had written countless letters to my parents, but Raj only allowed me to send one. He had dictated exactly what it would say. I thought about my sister and how she had laid in this very same room. Even the clothes I was now wearing belonged to her.

Raj had erratic mood swings. Some days he'd be kind, gentle, and loving, but others, he'd be depressed over losing Amara. Every single day, I'd hear him talking to someone so passionately and no one would be there. He'd mutter strange things under his breath and pace around the room at odd hours of the night.

"Where are you, my love? I didn't know it would kill you. I thought…you were stronger."

After crying myself to sleep every night, I knew I had to make peace with my new reality. I didn't try to run away because I knew Raj would find me. Even when I went outside, he knew. He always knew where I was.

I started to write another letter, but this time it was to my sister.

Dear Amara,

In the past two months that I have been here, I assumed I'd be upset with you. Why did you have to go off and die? Why couldn't you give him a son? Because if those answers were different from the reality, then I wouldn't be here. I'd be married to someone else and probably a lot happier. But I'm not upset with you about those things. I'm upset that you died and freed yourself from this life. I'm upset because I don't know what happened to you and how

you did it. I never wanted to live this life. I hate you and I hate myself but most of all, I hate him. Were you pregnant at any given time here? He slipped and said something that makes me think you were. I hope you weren't when you died. I wish you were still here, and not just because I wouldn't be living your life, but because I miss you. I miss Papa and the farm. But most of all, I miss me.

Love,
  Gia

Tucking the letter into the envelope, I slid it under my bed. My door creaked open, and I saw the white of his eyes in the small crack. Straightening my spine, I didn't know what to expect.

"Amara…"

Oh no. Whenever he called me Amara, that meant he wanted to be intimate. My husband always called me by my dead sister's name every single time we were together in bed.

"I'm not Amara. I'm not her! I will never be her." I winced.

Raj pushed the door open further and strode toward me.

"Amara, you know I had to protect you."

The scent of his aftershave grew more intense as he filled the space between us.

"Who did you have to protect her… I mean, me, from?" I pretended to be my sister.

Raj brushed his fingers through my hair and looked at me sadly. "Of course, you know who I had to protect you from…" He brushed his lips against to mine, which always triggered nausea inside me.

"I had to protect you from the evil." Kissing me aggressively, I felt light-headed.

CHAPTER
SEVEN

THE NEXT DAY, I felt dizzy from the extreme sleep-deprivation, considering I hadn't slept a wink with Raj clutching my waist and breathing in my face. He was whispering the strangest things that made no sense. Chanting words that sounded like Sanskrit, the ancient language of India. He wouldn't stop calling me Amara, and telling me that I'd forgive him one day. I waited for a sliver of the sun to pour in through the sheer, white curtains, and slid his arm off of me.

"Why aren't you happy here?" he asked with sleepiness lining his words. I couldn't help but laugh as I turned toward my small dresser, full of my sister's undergarments and nightgowns.

I closed my eyes and clutched the wooden drawer, thinking back to the moment I had walked through the front door of this tattered house.

I remembered my jaw dropping and eyes dripping with tears as he lifted me into his arms to carry me over the threshold, as if we were a normal, newlywed couple. As soon as I walked in, I sobbed, knowing I was so close to escaping. Anything would have been better than this. But he clutched my waist tightly and excitedly gave me a tour. Not much natural sunlight came in, and each room had aged, floral wallpaper in jewel tones, and most of the furniture was covered in yellowed, once-white sheets.

"Welcome home, my bride," he said proudly as the scent of dust and spices intertwined in a nauseating aroma.

"I thought your mother was bed-ridden?" I asked as I pointed to pots and pans stacked in the sink. I knew there was no way this man was cooking.

"She is. We have a chef. I'm a doctor, Gia," he boasted as I sunk my teeth into my bottom lip, suppressing my dry laughter.

The pride he felt in his title as a doctor, yet we lived as if we were in poverty. We hadn't passed a single house as we drove up the winding road to the secluded estate. I waited for the 'chef' to come, but they never did. Another lie. He was a liar, and my life was a lie—something I learned quickly. And this life was never mine to begin with. It was my sister's. The life she had always dreamt of quickly became her nightmare.

. . .

"Gia!" His voice startled me as my nails dug into the wood. I turned back toward him, but I didn't feel fear as he came close to me. I wasn't ovulating, so I knew he wouldn't touch me in the way that made my skin crawl.

"I want you to move into my bedroom from now on." He brushed his fingers through my hair and drew my face closer to his, pressing his forehead against mine. I hated the way I felt nervous, in a way that almost felt vulnerable of my conflicting emotions.

"Oh, it's okay… I'm grateful for my room." I tilted my head, trying to loosen his hand from my hair.

"Gia, you are my wife, and I am your husband. I'm… I'm sorry for how I have been. I'm sorry." He rubbed his lips against mine before pressing them against them and kissing me softly.

My heart was racing as he padded his fingers against the straps of my nightgown.

Kissing my neck, I couldn't help but let out a soft moan.

Why did it feel good? He never did this; he never kissed me this way. Even our wedding night was traumatic; he behaved in a way that I knew he was simply marking me.

Marking me as his property.

"Oh, Gia." He dropped my straps down and, because Amara's clothes were too big on me, the gown slid off with ease and pooled around my feet.

Lifting me in his arms, he carried me to the bed and laid me down. Looking at me, he parted my legs, and I closed my eyes, promising to not blame myself for what happened next.

I enjoyed having sex for the first time. I enjoyed having sex with the man who probably murdered my sister. I enjoyed having sex with him, maybe because he actually called me by my real name? Maybe because I craved some form of positive human interaction, and not feeling like I was a small mouse inching toward a trap? Maybe I was becoming the next case of Stockholm syndrome?

I hated myself completely.

That night, Raj carried me into his room after we were intimate and laid me into the plush, king-sized bed. His room was completely different from the rest of the house, renovated and clean, airy and light.

"This... this is beautiful." My voice was low as embarrassment still flooded through me, knowing Raj heard the way I cried out as an orgasm rippled through my entire body.

"I want us to be happy here. I will fix the house, Gia. I will give you the life I know you deserve, but I need a son. Please." He laid next to me as the moonlight cut through the window and reflected the deep caramel of his eyes.

"Okay," I whispered before closing my eyes, and for the first time, I didn't cloud my mind with thoughts on how to escape. I thought about how this was it.

I'd have to pretend I wanted this life and him—it was the only way I could buy myself time, not only to save myself, but to find out what happened to my sister. I knew he had probably done the exact same thing. He probably relaxed her, made love to her, and then promised lies all over again.

The difference was, I wasn't my sister. I wouldn't be stuffed into an urn before I had a chance to live. I wasn't the obedient wife like my sister was.

MY BODY WAS PLEADING for sleep but I couldn't shut off the intrusive thoughts or intense panic coursing through my body. Most of all, the unsettling echo had my heart racing. It was a banging, almost as if something was hitting against metal. I slid out of bed and looked out the window. Raj's room looked out to the abysmal forested area opposite the water. There was nothing but never-ending dense trees, then blackened waters on the other side. It was a fortress, secluded by the terrain, without neighbors or any form of traffic. I looked over my shoulder before tiptoeing out of his room. The house was dark with nothing but shadows dancing throughout. It didn't matter what time of day it was, the way the house was positioned meant the sun rose and fell against it. It was as if even the sun knew the house was already dead.

The cemetery that sat in the front was a reminder that Raj found some sick sense of pleasure in death. He was a medical examiner in the small nearby town, and then, he'd drive the bodies in his car—a hearse. My husband drove a hearse by *choice*. He'd offer free burial to those who would offer the bodies for science, and after he was done removing whatever he needed, he'd bury them.

I knew better, though. I had watched him through the window turning in with his shiny, black hearse up the gravel road and remove body after body from the back.

Closing my eyes, I thought back to the day I saw him. He had taken his shirt off and removed a corpse from the hearse. I remember my stomach tumbling as I watched him carry someone out. Someone with long blonde hair dangling down her frail shoulders. Dropping on his knees, he began talking to the body before cradling her. He laid with the corpse and pointed to the clouds, laughing and talking for hours. I stood there, hidden between the dusty curtains with my lips parted. I don't know if it were shock or disgust. Or maybe some sick fascination that this man and I lived together. We were married. I was married to a monster.

He eventually buried the body and laid wildflowers on top of the grave with such care that I almost believed he had some emotion inside of him.

But then, he came inside. I pretended to be asleep when really I had to gag myself with the corner of the blanket because I heard him. I heard Raj pleasuring himself in the bathroom. The moans that came from his mouth were more torturous than the internal screams I heard daily.

He wasn't doing anything for science, he was doing all of this for power and pleasure.

I wondered why no one asked to see the grave sites? Turned out, the bodies my husband would collect were those of the misfits. The ones who were unloved, never searched for, or unwanted.

My husband loved death the way most people loved life.

Gripping the black, steel banister, I walked down the stairs and each plank creaked below my bare feet. I questioned if my sister would have mentioned that in the letters she wrote, had Raj and her mother-in-law not been reading each word before she was allowed to send them. Three letters, that's all we got. They were full of lies, drawing out a beautiful, happy life of the American dream in black lettering.

I looked down at the itchy, blush-pink nightgown I was wearing. I hated these old-fashioned gowns, but it was all my mother had packed in my bag. They were her hand-me-downs and ran down to my ankles. Small flowers were embroidered all over, as well as stains of turmeric splashed all over that never came out when I hand washed my clothing in the small basin.

My head was pounding from the lack of sleep, and I couldn't remember the last time I had even a sip of water.

Making my way downstairs, a cast of light shimmered through the otherwise dark haze.

I looked around for the source, but couldn't see a single window open—each one was covered with heavy, maroon drapes. The scent of dust and spices made the nausea pool in my stomach as I looked around at the furniture covered with white sheets.

Standing at the stove, I placed the steel pot on the flame and poured water into it to make chai. Grabbing the fresh ginger, I began grating it rapidly while looking through the small, foggy window in front of me. A draft of cold air stung my exposed arms as I looked up for an air vent.

Nothing was there. Grating the ginger into the pot mindlessly, I felt it again.

Turning back, my eyes widened and the grater sliced against my fingers as I shrieked.

"Amara!" I stumbled back as I looked at the reflection in front of me. It wasn't my own, it was my sister's. The pot of water began bubbling as the flame grew larger. Her once glossy dark hair was knotted and dirty while her eyes were sunken in. A small smile grew on her face as she lifted her bony hand and wiggled her fingers at me. I could feel my own eyes rolling as my blood went cold.

"What are you doing?" Raj shouted as he pushed past me and turned the gas off.

I finally blinked and saw myself.

"I saw my sister in the window, but she wasn't outside. She… she…" I shook as I looked at Raj, who was eyeing me in shock as I turned and looked behind me wildly.

"Shut up," he said through clenched teeth as his fists tightened by his sides. Raj grabbed his keys and wallet and stormed out, slamming the door behind him. I walked to the door and peered through the half-moon window. The driveway was on the side, long and winding with seemingly no end. The gray clouds hung low as he made his way to the hearse and slid inside. His tires crunched against the gravel as he left.

My hand stung as I lifted it and examined my bloodied fingers. The grater had sliced off a layer of skin on my thumb. Grabbing a towel, I wrapped it and made my way to the small library hidden away. It was the only space in the entire house that I genuinely felt a sliver of peace in.

It was also the only place where the sun even dared to come inside in copious amounts. Sinking my knees into the sofa, I gripped the thick, gold velvet curtains and, in one swift motion, opened them, causing the dust to fly all around. Coughing, I choked on the dirtied air and sighed as I brushed my fingers against the book spines.

Wuthering Heights? I paused with my index finger brushed against the gold lettering. I had read it within three days when I first arrived.

How about *Pride and Prejudice*? No, I couldn't put myself through the strenuous distress that Mr. Darcy caused me. But then again, I could close my eyes and pretend Raj was Darcy.

Laughing out loud, I shook my head and stood as I looked at the rows and rows of medical textbooks.

My stomach churned as I looked at one, full of detailed images on surgery. Raj knew exactly how to heal someone, but most of all, he knew exactly how to kill someone without it being detected. He could make it look completely accidental. Shuddering, I shut the book and went back to the classics. I'd just close my eyes and pull one out—it didn't matter as long as I could get lost in the words and become anyone I wanted to be.

But as soon as I closed my eyes, the ceiling creaked as if footsteps were padding against the floor above.

Looking up, I stared at the grand crystal chandelier as I suppressed my breathing to be certain I wasn't just hearing something.

The crystals shook.

My lips trembled as I released my breath and heard the floor above me squeak with movement.

Sure, Raj's mother was upstairs, and the logical thought would be she was getting water or using the washroom, but she didn't walk.

She was paralyzed from the waist down.

"Hello?" I called out softly, perhaps just to comfort myself, knowing there wouldn't be a response.

"Raj..." My voice shook as I glided across the uneven, worn wooden floors with my gown lifting behind me as I turned and felt another gust of cold air. The ventilation in the house was poor to say the least, but the chill that would suddenly float around me felt unnatural.

"Mami?" I gripped the banister and looked up at the winding staircase. Silence.

When halfway up the stairs, I froze because the silence was fleeting and instead, replaced with the sound of running.

My entire body froze as I looked up at the ceiling. No one could have entered the house without me seeing them. Was his mother feigning her paralysis? I ran up the stairs and turned down the darkened hall.

Her door was open.

"Mami?" I sniffled as fear overtook my emotions.

A light snore was the only response I got. There was

no way someone could get into this house since the terrain was too daunting to climb. There was only one front door, which was always triple-locked. It had to be the aged-old air conditioning system that hardly worked or maybe the old pipes giving out. Walking closer, the small lantern flickered by her bedside. Her black hair was laced with silver and countless medications lined the nightstand messily.

Sinking down next to the small cot, I looked at her. When I had first moved into the home, I was terrified. Terrified of the man I slept next to who was now my husband. Terrified of the old, tattering house I'd spend the rest of my days in. Terrified that those days were running away from me by the second.

But taking care of Raj's mother gave me some form of normalcy. It's what I was intended to do according to my parents. Become a wife to the man they selected for me, take care of him and his family, and never object to anything they'd ask from me or of me. I was simply to live and breathe until my body gave out.

I looked at her deep wrinkles and wondered if she'd ever been happy. She, too, had an arranged marriage. She had one son, which was a victory of its own in the culture that consumed us all.

Slowly lifting my fingers, I brushed the straggling curl from her face, thinking of how much I oddly missed my mother.

I had sent them a few letters, just like Amara had, full of sugar-coated lies I had based around the fictional novels I'd grown to love. Raj read each one before he shoved it into an envelope and mailed it out. I'd cringe as I'd watch his tongue swipe across to seal it.

In two months, I called them once, though Raj didn't know at first. I had garnered the courage to take the landline and dial their number.

When it rang, my mother answered and didn't even sound excited. The first thing she asked me was, "Are you respecting Raj and his mother the way we raised you?"

My heart shattered. My dad took the phone from her and asked how I was, but I knew my mother was probably shooting daggers with her black-lined eyes. I pretended that the connection was giving out as I choked on my tears, feeling grief for my life.

Stroking Mami's hair in place as she snored blissfully, I thought about how strange it was to miss my mother when she never showed affection, though my father hardly did as well. There was no kissing or hugging. It was always stiff in the four walls where Amara and I constantly felt the burdens of being daughters.

Running my finger down Mami's cheek, I ground my teeth together and suddenly, her eyes flung open.

Sucking in a breath of air, I fell back and slapped my hand over my heart. Her once brown eyes looked almost hazel with the cataracts that had fogged them. Her thin, shriveled lips curved upward as a trail of drool dribbled from her mouth.

"Potha?" she rasped.

Grandson.

Swallowing the lump in my throat, I shook my head and forced myself up.

Turning her head slowly toward me, she smiled broadly.

"He will kill you. He'll slit your throat or take the life out of your lungs." Mami began laughing wildly while choking and coughing on her own saliva as fear rampaged through me.

Running out of her room, tears stung my eyes as I dropped down in front of the large oval mirror in the corner of my room.

Looking up at the girl in the reflection, I stroked my hand across my stomach.

"I don't want to die…" I whispered.

For the entire time I had been married to Raj, I thought I wanted to die, I thought of my life as a sand timer flipped over and running out.

But looking at myself, I wanted to live. I wanted to survive and leave this house. I wanted to go out and see the possibilities and beauties life could hold.

That *my* life could hold.

What if my only way out was to give Raj a child? He'd be content with the baby, so would his mother, and I... I could leave. I didn't have the motherly desire other women had. I could do it; I could abandon my child.

"HOW WAS YOUR DAY?" Raj looked up as he sliced into his dinner. He had prepared his own meal knowing I didn't know how to cook chicken as someone who had always been a vegetarian. But the way he moaned when he took a bite of it had my stomach flipping. It didn't look like chicken. It looked like intestines or something…human-like. The flicker of the candles illuminated his face as wax dripped down the sides like tears.

I was taken aback by his question. We'd never really conversed beyond aggressive conversations revolving around pregnancy and time running out.

Wiping my mouth, I cleared my throat. "Fine. Thank you." I shrugged.

"How was yours?" The simple three words and basic question was filled with awkwardness. I kept my eyes on my own plate as nausea coursed through me when I looked at the way he was eating his.

"It was nice." He replied. "Gia, I'm... I'm sorry I have been less than kind to you over these past two months." He brushed his hand over his tired scowl as my spine straightened. I didn't know how to process this sudden shift in character.

Parting my lips, I tried to piece the scattered words that fluttered in my mind together to make a coherent statement, but I couldn't.

"We don't need to try to have a baby right now. We can wait until you're ready." The usual lines that were deepened on his forehead with concern were non-existent as he spoke calmly.

Relief surged throughout my body as I blinked away the tears that stung my usually dry eyes.

"What?" My lips trembled.

Nodding, he stood and came around the eight-seater mahogany dining table. Each chair was uphol-stered with worn red and gold fabric, but it must have been beautiful once upon a time.

Sinking down on his knees by my chair, he placed my hand in his. "Gia, we have the choice to be happy. I know our marriage was arranged. I know we... well, you didn't have a choice. I know it must be terrifying to move across the world with a complete stranger, especially a man who was... was once married to your older sister. But I want us to have a normal, happy and beautiful life together. I'm tired, Gia. I'm tired of trying to appease my mother or our cultural standards and have a son. As long as I have you, I can wait." He paused as my hand shook in his. "With that said, I do want a child. I want a son... I need one, Gia. I..."

"Okay," I whispered. "I just... need time." I swallowed the lingering saliva in my mouth as peace surfaced inside me for the first time in months.

"I want to know what happened to my sister." I couldn't believe I was courageous enough to ask him, and part of me instantly regretted the blatant question. I was fearful he'd recognize the excitement I felt that he wouldn't harass me to have his child immediately.

"Gia." Raj sighed as he stood and brushed his hands against his pleated khakis.

"Two questions. You can ask me any two questions you want, and then you'll promise me we will focus on making what felt like a business transaction into a marriage." He waved me over as I slowly stood from the chair and followed behind him.

We walked into the library. I didn't want to be here with him; I felt possessive over this space in the otherwise dead estate. It was the only place I didn't feel like I was suffocating.

"What happened to Amara?"

Raj paused mid-air while taking a seat on the emerald-green velvet couch.

I sank into the single peeled cognac leather chair as his jaw ticked.

Exhaling loudly, he straightened his legs and walked over to the bookshelves. "My grandfather bought all of these." He brushed his fingers against the worn, yet vintage, books.

"He said it helped him learn English. But then, he became consumed by them. Making up these fabricated lies and stories. I hate fiction novels for that reason." Raj turned, the creases on his forehead deepening.

"Your sister is gone." Raj's lips tipped into a frown as I stared at him.

Wrapping my arms around my body, I whispered, "How?"

"Gia, she had a medical emergency. I couldn't save her and… you'd never be able to understand what really happened. I just need you, as my wife, to believe me when I say I didn't hurt her. I love… I loved her." Dropping his eyes to the wood floors, he sniffled and swiped his finger under his eye as tears began rolling down.

"I know it was wrong to call you by her name when we…" he started. Embarrassment pooled in my abdomen. "I was madly, truly, and deeply in love with your sister, and as much as it must pain you to hear, a part of me will always love her." Raj sat on the couch and scooted closer to me.

Gritting my teeth, I thought about my sister. I thought about how I couldn't believe I was married to the man who was still in love with her.

"Why didn't you let her call us?"

Raj brushed his hands across his face. "She didn't want to."

Furrowing my brows, I shook my head. "No, no… Amara would never have wanted to… abandon us and not talk to us."

Raj rested his chin on his palm and tilted his head slightly. "Amara wanted America to be her fresh start. She said you all would have used her for money or gifts. She thought she wouldn't be able to focus on our family if she kept in touch with yours."

"She loved us."

"Gia, how many times have you actually asked me to call your parents?"

I was taken aback. Was it true? Did I just forget about my parents because I was a world away from them now?

"I didn't think I was allowed to," I interjected. "You read my letters before I can even mail one."

"Gia, I am a physician. I can't have my wife making insane accusations in writing and mailing them across the world for your family to spread like fire with town gossip."

I hated how what he was saying had truth to it. I hated how…

A loud bash emitted from upstairs.

My eyes shot up to the ceiling but didn't stay there long. Instead, I followed Raj's line of vision and melted into the sofa.

"Raj…" I murmured under my breath as his face paled.

He had a large cut running against his forearm as blood began to pool out.

But just as I began to piece my mind together and try to stand to help him, a scratching against the wall had me grip the armrest.

In deep red, letters began to form.

SAVE

Raj gripped his bleeding arm and let out a cry as he clenched his eyes shut, as if he already knew what was coming. His screams grew louder as he fell to the ground and the veins in his forehead protruded more prominently.

I felt faint as I watched the letters appear against the yellowed wallpaper.

Lines were connected to form the rest, and the next word had chills covering my entire body

HER

Tears streamed down my cheeks as I blinked rapidly, hoping this wasn't happening. This couldn't be happening.

"Raj…" My voice didn't sound like my own. Brushing my neck, I began crying as the curtains flailed upward with a strong, cold gust of wind.

Shrieking out, Raj opened his eyes. "Go, Dakini! Go!" He began laughing hysterically as he stood and spun with the dusty curtains dancing. The books began falling off the shelves as the pages turned and everything began to blur.

The windows weren't opened, and the air conditioner barely worked. I pulled my knees to my chest and planted my face in between my shaking knees as my husband was laughing, screaming, and crying so piercingly that my ears began to ring. I sobbed into my legs, hoping tonight wouldn't be the night I died.

Raj collapsed again and began crawling on all fours towards me. His eyes streaked with red, his lips slammed together as a devious smile tipped his lips upward. "Dakini…"

My eyes grew wide as I saw a woman. Straggly black hair draped over her thin face and her body covered in a dirtied gown.

A small grin formed on her face.

"I don't want to die. Please." I whispered and slammed my eyes shut.

SUNLIGHT SHIMMERED in and the unusual warmth brushed against my face as I slowly opened my eyes.

Raj was on his knees with a bucket full of soapy water, running a sponge over the thick red letters that were now dripping down the walls.

My breathing shook as I looked at him and stood with weak knees. I swallowed the lump in my throat. "Raj…"

His hand stopped with the red-stained sponge, but he didn't turn toward me.

Letting out a sigh, his shoulders rolled downward. "You're awake."

Wrapping my arms around myself, I dragged my feet through the flattened carpet. "Yes."

I couldn't believe I had fallen asleep, but the heaviness of my head made me think Raj may have drugged me. Moving the sponge off the wall and sticking it into the bucket of water, he pressed his back against the wall. His shirt was stained crimson, and I looked at his arm, which was now wrapped in a gauze-like bandage.

"What...what happened?" I quivered as he stared at his soap-covered hands.

"Dakini," he rasped, his pupils dilating as he stared behind me. My spine tingled with a chill as I clenched my teeth together, terrified to turn around.

"Raj." I trembled as he stood and began to walk as if his body had no flexibility in it. Gripping the peeled banister, he turned and trekked up the stairs without another word.

"Dakini?" I whispered, spinning around and looking at the room full of books that I found so much comfort in while being alone, but now, I felt a presence. One that felt far too smothering.

I didn't know what to do or where to go. These four walls of the estate had become my entire world. The fear pooling inside me made me crave the comforting words of someone who loved me, cared for me, and wanted me to be safe. However, I didn't have that. My parents must have felt a burden lift off their shoulders now that both daughters were out of their lives. My husband, I scoffed at the word, was wrapped into the dangerous wrath something or someone was inflicting on him. My mother-in-law was decaying by the day, and I…

I was all alone.

I looked upstairs as the eerie silence taunted me more than the screams or the wicked laughter.

Grabbing the curved once-all black banister, I begrudgingly made myself up the stairs as each step creaked. My heart didn't race the way it usually did with each noise. After witnessing what I had the night before, perhaps I'd become oblivious to any further terror. I didn't want to stay emotionless because of this environment, but at the same time, I knew not opening my heart up would be the only form of protection I'd have here. I glanced over the ledge at Raj's bedroom. I walked into what I thought was my room, but my lips parted. It was emptied out. There was nothing there.

I knew he had wanted us to sleep together and share a bed, but to completely gut my one space in this otherwise hell?

Storming out, I made my way to Raj's bedroom, but immediately stopped in the doorway.

He was lifting a painting up and pinning it to our bedroom wall.

My heart thudded against my chest. It was a portrait of… Amara. She looked beautiful. It was taken outside, down by the ocean. Raj told me we couldn't go down there, insisting it was unsafe.

Amara was wearing a bhindi on her forehead, bangles around her wrists, and a beautiful beaded white saree as she laughed and looked off at the ocean.

She looked happy.

"Raj…" I breathed out as he continued to hang the image with care. I noticed my small dresser was now in the room, along with my limited personal items neatly lined on the vanity.

"Hello, Amara," he hummed and turned toward me.

No. My eyes filled with tears. I couldn't take this, not when I needed him to help me understand what demonic spirit or entity was clearly lurking within these walls. Not when I needed him to be my one person in the entire world to help me want to breathe.

"Look." He smiled and pointed at the photo. "Do you remember this day, my love? It was the day we found out. I still can't believe you're back. I begged for you to come back and see our life. You never realized how beautiful it was." He nodded as he cupped my face within his dry, cracked palms.

My stomach twisted in knots as I looked at the blood-stained gauze wrapped around his arm. "Raj, I'm not her. I'm not Amara."

"Do you remember?" he crooned while tucking in a strand of hair behind my ear.

Suddenly, it occurred to me. I had to be her; it was the only way I could figure out what was happening.

"No, my dear. I don't remember," I choked out as I dropped my eyes to the ground.

He brushed his hand against my stomach, and that is when I knew.

My sister was pregnant.

"It was the day we found out. But it was such a short-lived happiness because you just had to be a whore." A small smile tipped across his face, and my breathing stopped.

What had my sister done?

RAJ LAID next to me in what was now 'our' bed and rested his head against my stomach. My mind was racing.

Raj traced my skin as he kissed my abdomen. "We were so close, weren't we?" He smiled up at me as his pupils dilated. "We will try again and again until our family is complete."

A loud bang echoed, but Raj didn't even flinch. He just hummed and continued tracing words I couldn't figure out against my flesh.

"What is that?" I whispered as the clanking grew louder. The stillness and silence between us as the clear echo didn't even bother him made me even more concerned. "Raj, how did those words... How did someone cut your arm?"

· · ·

Looking up at me, he shook his head. "I wrote those words, silly woman. I cut myself and wrote those words. You didn't see me do it because you were too busy trying to make this life seem like some horror movie. I want you to give me my baby; I need you to give me a son. But you won't, so I decided to scare you. It was wrong, I know. I'm sorry, my love."

No... I saw the letters form on the wall with Raj sitting across from me. I saw the wind pick up, the screeching and the world shift in front of my eyes. I felt a dark presence.

"Idle minds lead to insanity, Amara." He rolled over as I stared at the ceiling. Was he right? Was I losing my mind? Did he cut his arm? Had I dazed out?

The night fell and darkness took over our bedroom. Shadows danced as the curtains twirled with the howling wind. I could hear the ocean grow more powerful as the waves crashed against the boulders below.

Raj was snoring lightly next to me, the puttering of his lips while his nose flared slightly, which drove me crazy. I felt overly warm with the ceiling fan cutting through the dry air. Creaking echoed, and I looked toward the door as it slowly opened. My body grew still as I held my breath and widened my eyes. A shadow dripped in, but I couldn't see anyone behind it. Sweat grew at the nape of my neck. "Raj…" I nudged his arm as the door began to open wider.

"Gigi." Her voice echoed lowly. My palms grew moist as my body tightened. There was only one person in the world who called me 'Gigi,' and it was my older sister. I didn't blink for fear that if I did, I would miss something. That I wouldn't see her.

Sliding out of bed slowly and placing my feet on the ground, I hoped I could steady myself as my legs trembled with each step forward.

"Amara?" I called out in a hushed whisper. The shadow began to retreat, but I was too scared and couldn't walk any faster.

With one foot forcefully in front of the other, I clutched myself as the shadow grew smaller and more distant.

Opening the door slowly, the screeching of the rusted latches felt like nails on a chalkboard. Blinking once, I leaned out the doorframe but then…

"Hello, Gigi," the voice rasped. The white of Raj's mother's teeth and eyes cut through the darkness.

"Mami!" I screamed and tumbled back. She sprinted away down the hall with her back curved and gown flying behind her. Her footsteps pounded against the wood floors as I froze in place paralyzed by shock and terror.

"Gia?" Raj was now behind me, spinning me around with tired eyes.

Turning the light on, I exhaled and crumbled to the floor with long, heavy breaths as if I had run miles.

"What is happening?"

"She was running… Your mother… was…" I choked out as Raj dropped to his knees in front of me.

"Gia, my mother has been paralyzed from the waist down for years. She has been bedridden with no interest in even sliding into a wheelchair, let alone running." Raj shook his head and stood. All I could hear was a door opening and closing as I turned my body and laid on the side.

"I knew this day would come. It happened to her, too. Your parents cursed me with two mentally unwell brides." He stalked across the floor and grabbed my arm.

Lifting my eyes upward, I shook my head. "No, Raj. No!" I screamed as his nails dug into my skin harder and he lifted the needle, injecting it straight into my vein.

Within seconds, I felt like I was in a tunnel, my eyes growing hazy, his voice sounding distant, and his touch feeling foreign.

I watched my feet being lifted and my body being dragged out of our bedroom and down the hall. Was this it? Would Raj kill me? Was I watching my own death as if it were a movie scene. I hadn't even lived yet, and now it was all over. A small grin grew across my face.

I was relieved.

CHAPTER
TWELVE

COLD WATER BRUSHED against my feet as seagulls crooned. *I was dead.* I never truly believed in reincarnation, which was embedded into my beliefs from the moment I was born. I suppose I didn't believe in it because I wondered what kind of sins I had done in a previous life to be born as a girl in India where it was perceived as a burden. What would my life have been like had I been born a man? A man who was idolized simply because of dated customs. Had I been reborn? Or was this the afterlife?

The fresh air felt glorious as I inhaled the salty scent and slowly opened my eyes. I was staring up at a boulder. I was inside one? Where was I? I carefully turned my sore neck and looked to the side… more stone.

"She's awake." A familiar voice that elicited a nauseated sensation ricocheted in the cave.

My throat felt scaly as I looked down and saw I was laying on some form of slat. Florals decorated it and a fire crackling close by, and when I looked in front of me, the ocean was teasing the opening.

"Amara." The voice sounded so much like my mother's, laced with a thick Indian accent.

A woman dressed in a deep orange gown appeared by my side. Her neck was draped with a long, beaded necklace, while her black hair was left in frizzy waves. The dark, smudged eyeliner around her eyes made the whites stand out all the more.

"Amara," she repeated, lifting her wrinkled, caramel hand in front of my face. Fear coursed through my body, but I couldn't move.

I was paralyzed. Had I fallen? Did Raj break my legs?

"Bring the salt," she barked. Wincing, I turned my head to follow the sound of the puttering footsteps.

Raj. My husband was wearing a long white tunic with thin, baggy white pants. A deep red mark was on his forehead as he rummaged through a table filled with bottles and books.

Lifting a jar in his hand, he raced over without looking at me.

The woman grabbed it from him and poured a blend of salt and other substances into her hand before leaning to me. "Close your eyes. You can't see the evil leaving your body." Her thin, cracked lips dipped into a frown.

I did as I was told. But as she began chanting in Sanskrit, my body began to shake, and I opened them slightly. Her hands were moving wildly over my body as she clutched the salt in her hands, then she ran toward the mouth of the cave and threw the salt into the ocean before dropping to her knees and shrieking.

Raj ran over to me and grabbed my hands. "Amara!" He nodded desperately.

"I'm not her," I sobbed as my body felt lighter. "Please don't make me be her. I can't do it."

"What is your name, child." The woman came back with tears draining from her eyes.

"Gia. Amara… was my sister." I swallowed the minimal saliva that was in my mouth.

The woman's eyes shot up to Raj. Shaking her head at him, she looked angry. "I'm Kali ma." She brushed her palm against my forehead. "You won't live long. She will get you." Spinning around, her orange gown floated behind her as she walked to the edge and sat in a meditative pose. "The evil eye has left her. She is fine for now."

Raj sighed and slid his hand under my back. "Let's go. We must return home. Mami needs us back." My legs were weak but finally had movement. Raj lifted me and tugged my arm around his shoulder.

"Don't listen to her. I won't let you die." His eyes locked onto mine as my cheeks filled with warmth.

What my husband didn't know was that was such a punishment. I wanted to die. I wish I had. What kind of life was this?

I turned my head towards Kali ma. Did she live here? It was a common belief in India that nazaar also known as evil eye could cause one to fall ill, become mentally unstable and even die. Those with superior powers like priests or elders could rid the evil. But I didn't feel any different. I felt more fear. Raj wanted me to live. I'd have preferred he let me die.

I sat on the small stool next to Mami's bed. She was moaning in pain as I dipped the sponge into the basin full of warm water. She was deteriorating. In the midst of having to clean her when she soiled herself or when she'd shoot me looks of disapproval, I'd pray under my breath that she'd just die already. However, she seemed indestructible. She lived such a sad life, yet her body still hadn't given out.

"Your son ruined my life," I breathed out, shocked by my words to the woman in front of me.

Indian culture taught us to respect our mothers-in-laws, no matter how strict, harsh, or toxic they could be. We were raised to believe they knew best, even if it was wrong.

But what would this woman do? She only spoke every so often, and usually only to spit out cruel jabs about my hair or appearance.

She shot her angry eyes to my stomach. "Give him a son."

Pulling my cardigan closer together, I threw the sponge into the water and tried to back away, but her hand stretched out and slapped around my wrist, tugging me closer. I was taken aback by her strength.

Opening her mouth, she paused and smiled at me.

"You stupid, little girl… Your only way out is to give him a son."

My heart was racing. My way out?

"If I give him a son, he'll let me leave?" I questioned as her grip tightened.

Nodding, she began to laugh. "She will take him, too!" She began screaming and jamming her finger into my abdomen.

"Ah!" I cried out and swatted her hand off me. Tumbling back, the stool screeched against the wood as I sprinted out of the room. My head felt light as the events that had transpired over the past few days had my mind in a darker place than I thought was possible.

Gripping the banister, I looked down at the winding staircase.

This estate was centuries old. Had anyone jumped? Dark thoughts clouded my mind as I walked down and realized the hearse was gone. Raj must have gone to work.

My stomach growled, and I couldn't remember the last meal I had eaten. Looking out of the fogged kitchen window, I watched the never-ending ocean. I wanted to go back to Kali ma. I wanted to find her, and ask her if she knew anything about Raj and his family. Had she met my sister? When we walked back on the unforgiving boulders, climbed a small dirt path up, I tried to memorize the route but my head was far too heavy. What would I do if I trekked down the cliff and didn't find it? I'd be out there, alone, with no food, water, or a way to reach help.

I opened the small metal tin and pulled a dry roti out and placed it on a plate. We didn't even have spicy pickle to eat it with, and Raj hadn't brought home any fresh vegetables for me to cook. We'd been eating plain rice and lentil soup lately, and with the little whole wheat flour I had found—that had clearly been chewed by mice—I made roti to hopefully fill my stomach longer.

Lost in my thoughts, I began chewing the hard, cold bread, looking at the water when the phone rang.

Jolting, I spun around and stared at the small, pale-yellow landline that was attached to the dated floral wallpaper.

No one had called, not even my parents. I had called them once, but that was all. Looking up at the ceiling, I wondered if Mami could hear the ringing? Placing my plate down, I lifted the phone.

"Hello," I answered, my heart pounding against my chest, hoping it wasn't Raj. He had warned me that if I ever used the phone, especially to call the police, they'd take me to a shelter for women where dangerous things happened. Clearly, I knew the irony of it all. But I was an immigrant, a foreigner; I knew I wouldn't survive out there with no money, no family, and not even a single friend.

On the other end of the line, heavy breathing ensued.

"Hello?" I repeated, my voice dropping.

"Gia."

Her voice was just as sweet as it had always been.

Swallowing and exhaling, I clutched the phone. "Amara?"

CHAPTER
THIRTEEN

MY HANDS SHOOK as I clutched the phone.

"Amara?" My voice cracked as I thought about the simple name I had said thousands of times in my life. I closed my eyes and repeated my older sister's name. "Amara?"

Heavy breathing followed.

"Please, please… talk to me. I… I need you to talk to me." My lips trembled as tears seeped out of my eyelids.

"You need to get out of that house. Dakini won't rest until you give him a son. But I need you to find…" There was a crackle.

"Where are you? How are you…" I trailed, but just as I rushed to say more, the line buzzed.

She hung up.

Sinking to the floor, I clutched my legs to my chest.

My sister was alive? Where was she? How did she leave…

Suddenly, I could hear Mami hacking. Pressing my palms against the tiled floors, I stood and quickly got her jug of water and a small cup before walking upstairs. But just as my hand gripped the cool brass doorknob, I stopped. She was speaking to someone. Or rather, she was singing to someone.

"Chanda hai tu, meri suraj hai tu…"

You're my moon, you're my sun.

Who was she singing to? Opening the door, I froze. Mami was on the floor, singing next to the small air vent.

"Mami!" She had to have fallen.

Cursing at me in Hindi to help her without her body moving, I trembled. The stench of the room had me holding my breath. I knew I should have been better at caring for her—I hardly cleaned her room, and the bedsheets were long overdue to be changed. But lifting her up on my own was exhausting. I had to convince Raj we needed to hire someone like a nurse to help us. Guilt panged me as I rolled the wheelchair over and used every ounce of strength to lift her into it. My back and arms hurt as I pushed her to the window and opened it. The dust blew inward as the cold ocean air slapped my face. "Who were you singing to, Mami?" I asked cautiously as she stared out the window as the curtains danced with the howling wind.

I scrunched my nose as I peeled off the bedsheets and blankets. Urine and feces stains were imprinted. Three bedpans lingered and I was full of shame. She wasn't my mother, yet here I was, carrying the burden of care while her son was more concerned with a life we hadn't created yet than the one withering away in his home.

Mami stared out the window as her eyes began to close. She was slumped over, and I realized she was looking at her hands.

"Beti," she rasped.

Daughter.

I shook my head. "What? I don't understand, Mami. I don't understand who you are talking about."

"Give us a son," she rasped.

No one loved me. It was a realization I thought I was okay with, but no, I wasn't. My parents didn't love me enough to say no to sending me across the world with a man who was with my sister when she died. My husband didn't love me, but rather, was obsessed with said dead sister. My mother-in-law only looked at me as a pawn in her hopes to have a grandson. What was I even living for? A mere idea of what I could potentially have as a life?

"Please, Mami, tell me what happened to my

sister," I pleaded as she stared out through the billowing curtains.

Mami craned her neck and widened her eyes as she looked at me. She screamed, "You! You killed her!"

I tumbled back, slapping my hands over my ears as they rang from the sudden high-pitched shrieks.

Shaking my head, I choked on my own sobs. "No! No, I didn't!"

I ran out of the room and straight into him.

His arms wrapped around me as terror and anxiety rippled through me. I didn't know why I felt like I was living through some out-of-body experience.

Had I already died?

"Gia, Gia..." His voice was oddly comforting as I allowed him to hold me. His fingertips dug into my hips as he pulled me closer, and I slowly looked up at him. Furrowing his thick brows, he tilted his head. "Are you alright?" His voice was laced with concern, but just as he leaned closer to my face and brushed his thumb against my lower lip, the door behind us slammed shut.

"Oh my god, Mami!" I exclaimed as Raj pushed behind me, attempting to open the door. Except, it wouldn't open. The door was locked.

I slapped his hands away, knowing I didn't lock it. I had left Mami in her wheelchair by the window.

It opened. Gasping, I felt faint. Mami was tucked

away in her bed, deep asleep. The sheets were on and the pile I had left was still there.

"Did you leave the wheelchair out? Always keep it by the bed." Raj carefully closed the window before rolling the wheelchair back to the bedside.

"Raj…" My voice broke as I felt a shiver shoot up my spine. "Can Mami… walk?"

Raj looked over at me before bending and compiling the dirtied bedding, then carried it out and waved me with him.

"Gia… what is going on with you?" He shook his head. "Mami has been paralyzed for decades. She… she can barely speak, let alone walk. Please just…" Lifting his hand, he pleaded with his eyes for me to stop.

I exhaled, knowing there was no way my mind was playing tricks on me. I left her in the wheelchair. I hadn't changed her bedding… I…

I was exhausted.

I crossed my arms and straightened my back. "I'd like to call my parents."

Raj loosened his shoulders as he froze mid-way on the stairs. "Okay. After you bathe tonight, you may call them." He nodded and jogged down the rest of the stairs.

The tightness in my chest felt lighter. I was proud of myself for asking a simple question that most wives wouldn't have to ask permission for. I didn't know what was sadder—being happy I could talk to the parents who put me in the situation or feeling gratitude toward the man who was keeping me in it?

I STOOD under the hot water. Usually, the water ran cold, so it was a relief to feel it actually comfortable. The steam surrounded me as I scrubbed with the sliver of soap that was melting away. I began to hum the same song Mami was singing, thinking of how my sister would sing it to me.

Opening my eyes slowly, the overly-floral scented shampoo stung my eyes. But before I slammed them shut, I forced myself to look. A butterfly was drawn into the steam. I took a step back.

The bathroom door creaked and suddenly, a figure appeared as I clutched my arms around myself, cowering as the water splattered louder against the empty space.

The lights shut off, and I held my breath.

Closing my eyes, I couldn't take the level of fear

that was coursing through my naked body. I felt even more vulnerable now.

The shower door opened as my back pressed against the cold wall.

"My love…"

It was Raj. My husband was coming into the shower with me. Opening my eyes, I could feel his body grow closer to mine.

"I'm so sorry about everything." My heart was pounding against my chest as his fingers raked over my body. Why was this so awkward when Raj was my husband? The lights were off, yet I'd never felt more embarrassed being naked without blankets or sheets to hide under.

"Our wedding night… drugging you and being so distant with you when I knew this had to be the scariest thing any woman could do in her life. Marrying a complete stranger, leaving your parents, and assuming that I… I did something to Amara." He didn't stop speaking, it was as if he knew this was his last chance to convince me otherwise.

"Gia, we get one life to live. One. I do not want to waste it or have you living in fear when I am innocent. I didn't hurt her. I promise you. She died, and a part of me will never stop loving her. Gia, I know this is hard for you to hear, but Amara was the love of my life. I can't explain it, but she was. I loved her and she loved me. The truth is, when she died, I think a piece of my soul died, and I used my anger and grief to hurt you. But you, my beautiful Gia, are my wife, and I... and we can learn to love each other. Amara and I were strangers and so are we, but now it's time for us to love, respect, and laugh together." Raj paused and pulled me toward the water. My quivering body immediately reacted with relief as the hot pellets grazed my skin.

"I don't think I can," I whispered with sheer honesty.

Pursing my lips, hoping I wouldn't cry, I repeated myself, "I... don't think I can love you or believe that you didn't do something to Amara."

Raj wrapped his arms around me. "Let this water cleanse you, and know that you do have a choice. The choice you have is either to pretend to love me until your mind believes it, or live a life of fear, hatred, and false hoods. I don't want to be the husband who blackmails his wife, but just know the farm that is now thriving back in your small village and keeping your parents stomachs full and a roof over their head is only due to my generosity. Think, you'd be married off to some controlling man in India with a demanding mother-in-law and extended family watching your every step. Here, you can dance, read, enjoy my company without a second thought." I looked up at Raj seeing the whites of his eyes grow. "Dakini."

"Letters written in blood, random noises, shadows… Raj, I'm scared. I…"

"I've let my mother and our culture get the best of my intelligence. I was convinced this home was a death trap. As a physician, I know there is a level of science versus supernatural, and yes, there is darkness embedded in this house, but don't you think darkness is combated by light, and light is brought in by love?" Both palms cradled my face as he pressed his head against mine. The water began to run cold as he murmured, "I have a proposal for you."

I scoffed at the thought of a proposal from the man I was married to but, in fact, never actually proposed. I'd seen some American films where the man drops down on one knee after an epic love story. I'd dream of slapping my cheeks in shock as he lifted the ring to my finger and spun me around. But that wasn't in the cards for me. I'd never experience that.

"Okay," I whispered.

"Let's pretend we aren't married. Let's go on a date. Let's… start our story the way you'd dream of."

My lips parted in shock as I wiped the now-cold water from my face. What was happening? Part of adulthood is having the realization that reality is, in fact, far less sweet than the dreams we had always wanted. Part of adulthood is having the realization that life is simply a cycle of the same day, over and over again, until we die. It was true; I was stuck here with no escape. I was terrified of everything. I didn't know anyone. My accent stuck through each word like honey. I had no money, no education that could translate into a job here. I... I was married to a doctor, living in a house of terror with a paralyzed mother-in-law, and no one who genuinely cared if I was alive or dead.

Except... maybe Raj. Maybe he was using me as a scapegoat for his pain over losing my sister. Maybe she really did just... die.

Supernatural things haunted this house, the phone call... Maybe it was some form of black magic that someone had plagued us with. Was our pain and sadness really a sponge for this to evolve into a haunting?

I knew we could do a religious ceremony to settle the spirits—I'd seen it done countless of times back in India. But what kind of spirit was this? What or rather, who was Dakini?

"What do you think, Gia? Will you go on date with

me tomorrow night? It's Friday… I hear it's beautiful in the city lately."

"Yes." I would get to leave this place for even a few hours. I could see what was out there. I could, in fact, create more options for myself, or maybe simply come to the realization that it was true.

I had none.

"MA, I saw actual letters in bloo—" I clutched the phone to my mouth. Raj allowed me to call my parents in total privacy the next morning while he was at work.

"It must be Amara's spirit. She's not resting because she's worried about you. How you're behaving ungratefully and… childish, Gia," my mother spewed out with anger. "You need to light the candle and say a prayer. Slice lemons, hang peppers, and chant to let her soul rest. I hope you're also taking care of Raj and his mother. Do not embarrass our family, Gia. How are Raj and his mother?"

My heart ached for the little girl inside me who always craved her mother's approval, who always desired a mother who worried about her over random people in the "society" that meant more than family.

But at the same time, I was sad for the girl who

became a woman who was still too scared to speak up and break the cycle.

"I'll do the prayer, Ma. Raj and his mother are well," I choked out with full realization that she didn't once ask how I was doing.

"Amara's spirit needs to rest, and if after you've done what I have told you and there are still disturbances, then that means you've allowed black magic to creep inside your home. There are other solutions, but we won't get into it now," my mother sternly warned. I knew all about black magic—I grew up fearful of it. Evil eye, unsettled spirits, cursed land... we were taught and told endless stories about it occurring to people we loved, even killing them.

"Ma, I want to come home." I winced, as if saying the simple sentence pained me. No matter how toxic parents could be, something about speaking to them inflicted this child-like regression to rear its head.

"You don't have a home to come to. That is your home. Look at your sister; the only way she came back to us was in an urn. Enough, Gia. You live in America. How many girls your age in our village would trade places with you in a heartbeat?" My mother's voice raised. "Do the prayer, and do not call me again with rubbish."

. . .

I began weeping, covering my mouth so she wouldn't hear her daughter breaking or being a human with actual emotions. "Can… I talk… to Papa?" I pushed through.

"No, I don't want to worry him. Gia, while you may think you're the only person struggling while you live a glamorous life in America—the life your grateful sister should have been living—your father and I are destroying our bodies every day managing the farm. Your papa collapsed. Did you know? He collapsed." I tugged the cord of the phone so it would come down with me as I buckled into the floor.

"Is he okay?" I sobbed, not caring if she heard how weak I was.

"No, Gia, he's not okay. I need you to ask Raj to send us…"

Money. My mother wanted me to ask the husband I hardly knew for money to send to them.

"Gia, beta… you know we have done so much for you. And then we lost our daughter."

I'm still here, Ma.

"I'll talk to him. Please tell Papa…" Tell him what? That I loved him? I loved my mother. We never said those three words; we never expressed emotion beyond expectation.

"Your auntie is calling, I have to go. Bye." I parted my lips, but before I could even speak, she had hung up.

I looked around the old kitchen. I wasn't living a glamorous life; I was living in a tattered secluded fortress on a cliffside, plagued with pain.

Pushing myself off the tiled floor, I glanced at the time. Raj told me he'd leave work at two, and we could leave around four for a night out in the city. I needed to go check on Mami, and with one glance in the mirror, I knew I had to spend time getting ready. Most days I wore Amara's old gowns and random pieces of clothing I'd put together. We hadn't gone shopping; I never had left these four walls beyond waking up next to the ocean. I had made peace that, back in India, I was in a different prison, and now I was tired of this house being another. I knew what I needed to do.

I had to trick my husband into falling in love with me.

———

Soap and water stung my skin as blood trickled down my leg. I had found a half-rusted razor under the sink. Raj took away the one I had when I first moved here, thinking I'd slit my wrists and kill myself.

He wasn't necessarily wrong…

Truthfully, I daydreamed of the days where I was lying in a pool of my own blood with my life flashing in front of my eyes.

But then, what would stop me from doing it—considering I could have used a kitchen knife. I realized I actually did want to live. For what? A chance at seeing the world through my own eyes versus the lenses that were covering them my entire life. For whom? For myself—the one person I never got to prioritize.

I watched the blood swirl into the water. It was beautiful. Life was so very fragile. One wrong cut, and I could take away my breath forever.

Shaking my head, I sighed and turned the rickety shower head. I climbed into the clawfoot bathtub and stood. Rubbing the thin bar of soap all over my body, I placed it down before taking the top off the cheap, floral-scented shampoo and squeezed it into my palm. My thick black hair was coated in oil, and I scrubbed it out as best as I could before washing my entire body.

The water was warm, but suddenly, as I was lost in my thoughts, it became hotter. The steam immediately built like a thick cloud around me. I gasped as I reached to open the glass door, but it wouldn't budge. My skin began burning as the droplets scorched my skin.

My breath hitched as I clenched my jaw and slammed my hands against the door.

But suddenly, I didn't feel anything.

In front of my eyes, a small butterfly was being traced into the steam.

"Amara, please help me...." I cried out, and just like that, I pressed against the door and tumbled out. My caramel skin was streaked red as I pressed my palms into the tile and coughed violently.

My sister was here.

Was my mother right? My soft-spoken sister couldn't rest because she saw me living her life in pain?

Peeling myself off the floor, I swiped the steam off the small bathroom mirror and choked on air.

The girl in the reflection wasn't me...

It was Amara, and she was looking right at me.

Slamming my fist against the mirror, I screamed, "Amara!" I repeated the action until my fists grew raw and bloodied and the mirror shattered in front of my eyes.

Flinging around, no one was there.

I turned back slowly and saw myself.

I was losing my mind. More than Raj, more than Mami, or the unsettled spirits tainting this house—the person I was most scared of was the one staring back at me.

My mind was the only weapon I had, and here I was, allowing it to become weak.

The only way I knew I could protect myself was to lie to myself. Force myself to believe that Raj was a loving husband, that this house could be a home, and that I was… fine.

Maybe while attempting to make my husband love me, I could find a way to love this life, too.

AFTER LATHERING my face with coconut oil, lining my eyes using the small stub of eyeliner I had left, and coloring my lips in the deep maroon I took from my sister's collection, I stood and did a small spin.

I didn't have anything else to use, yet I felt beautiful. More beautiful than I had in the months I had lived here, and maybe, for now, that was enough.

Brushing my hands against the knee-length red dress I had found buried in the back of Amara's belongings, I loosened my shoulders as I gripped the banister and made my way downstairs.

I had already checked on Mami, brought her food, and elevated her pillows. She wouldn't look at me, but I knew she was awake. As soon as I walked in, her eyes widened when she saw me, and she immediately slammed them shut again. I hated how she didn't have the heart to say something as simple as, "You look nice."

I hated how I craved that affirmation from someone that should have loved me.

Checking the time, I knew Raj would be here any minute. I looked down at my fingernails, wishing I had nail polish, but the shine of my engagement ring made me realize how I wasn't Amara. He did want more for me. He never gave my sister a diamond ring, just a simple wedding band. But for me, he bought this. Looking around the library, I smiled at my safe space.

Tugging *Pride and Prejudice* out from the bookshelf, I sank into the couch and flipped through to the dog-eared page I had left on. I was lost in the story and grinning ear-to-ear when a voice cleared.

"My love." His eyes glistened as he stood with his arms behind his back with a small smirk across his face. He was wearing a suit, his hair was neatly brushed, and he looked…

Moving closer to me, his eyes dropped down my entire body as I stood and placed my book on the small end table.

"You are making it hard to breathe, darling wife, for you have stolen my breath."

. . .

My lips parted as I watched his eyes trace my body as he held his hands behind his back steady. Warmth grew in my cheeks as I swallowed. "I… I didn't have much makeup, and this…" I brushed my hands against the somewhat wrinkled dress that hung loosely over my frame.

"It's perfect. You are perfect."

Was it possible to have a blank slate? Was it possible for me to forget the aggressive behavior Raj depicted, or the way he had called me by my sister's name countless times while being intimate?

Was it possible for me to convince myself that this was the only way I'd survive?

"Thank you. You look very nice." I averted my eyes. He didn't say anything, but rather pulled his arms out from behind and handed me a bouquet of flowers with a butterfly pick.

I stared at them before looking up at Raj. "Why did you choose this?" I whispered.

"Your necklace." He pointed to the small butterfly around my neck.

Closing my eyes and brushing my fingers against it, I smiled. "Thank you." I took the flowers from him and quickly put them in the kitchen before following him outside. The sun was setting, and I squinted. I hardly saw the sunlight. In the months I had lived here, I had never left this area.

I had never gone to a store, a restaurant; I had never interacted with anyone beyond Raj, his mother, and… Kali ma. I shuddered.

"Shall we?" Raj opened the door for me and waved me into the car.

The hearse.

Hesitating, I slid into the car.

My heart raced as the car's stench stung my noise.

I couldn't let this be the moment where Raj finally decided I'd continue to make his life hard. After all, my husband drove a hearse, but at least I got to sit in the front seat and not lay in the back… for now.

My stomach twisted as soon as Raj started driving down the winded pathway. It had been so long since I had sat in a car. I watched the dense trees blur past us as my body shook from the gravel crunching underneath the worn tires.

"How was your phone call with your parents?" Raj asked softly.

I looked back towards him. He truly was a handsome man. The perfect, chiseled jawline with neatly trimmed hair, and the suit he was donning fit his body like a glove. If I had never known anything about him and saw him in passing, I was sure I'd have taken a second look.

"It went well. Raj… I told my mother about the… well, strange things that have happened in the house, and she thinks it's Amara's soul. She thinks we need to hire a priest and have the house prayed over."

Raj's jaw ticked. I scrunched my nose as the stench of the car felt overwhelming again. "Can I roll my window down?" Raj looked over at me with his brows lowered, quickly pressing something that caused a clicking noise.

He had locked the windows.

"No."

Sliding it off, I nodded and looked ahead. "We can ask the priest to come to the house if you think it would help," he added.

"It's humid out, I can't risk the interior of my car; that's why I said no to opening your window, my love." My eyes widened and my body felt as if it had become a statue.

Moving one hand off the steering wheel he opened his palm and placed the back of his hand on my thigh. My breathing grew erratic, and I hated that I was inhaling the malodorous scent so quickly, simply because I couldn't get my nerves under control.

I didn't know what I was supposed to do.

"Will you hold my hand?" Raj glanced over at me with a smirk drawn across his lips.

Sliding my shaking hand into his, I stared down as he intertwined his fingers with mine. "You are so much like her, but at the same time, nothing like her at all."

He cleared his throat and made a turn. I started to see shops and buildings. We lived closer to the city than Raj ever let me know.

"I'm nothing like her." I don't know why the words came out harsher than I meant to say them. Perhaps, because, I was always compared to my soft-spoken, obedient sister.

"You're right. You are even better, stronger." He tightened his hand around mine and lifted it before dipping his head down and kissing the back of my hand.

My breath hitched as I immediately looked away, full of embarrassment that my husband was showing affection. That my husband thought I was better than my sister, his first wife.

"Then why did you call me her name? Even on our wedding night? Every single time we…"

"Because I was in love with her and she… she left me. She promised she'd be by my side, even when she found out about…" Raj stopped abruptly and released my hand.

"Found out about what?"

"Gia, this is our first date. I am begging you to let us start living our life as husband and wife. Please." Raj sounded exhausted.

"Do you not smell the…" I began, but Raj looked over at me with his eyes full of hope. Hope that I'd let it all go. That he could wave a wand and tell me sweet nothings and I'd fall in love with him.

I had to pretend to love him. I knew this was the only solution I now had in order to gain his trust. In order to gain my own sense of freedom.

"I'm sorry. I'm excited for our date and so grateful that you planned it. I'm sorry, Raj. I think I just want to have the priest come, and maybe we could… clean and redecorate the house a bit? Make it our home." I nodded at him with a forced smile.

His eyes lit up as his lips twitched into a grin.

Stupid man.

"I agree, the house has needed a woman's touch and we—" he cut himself off.

"Amara and you were going to renovate it?" I finished his sentence for him. "It's okay if you talk about her, you know. Although, I think we have so much to learn about us the one thing in common we have with certainty is that we both loved my sister."

Raj rolled his lips together before letting out a long sigh. "With time, Gia, I think the one thing we will have in common with certainty is our mutual love for one another."

I had prepared myself, I told myself I could fake it. I could pretend to love my husband, but now, in this moment, why did everything start feeling blurry. Why did my heart suddenly feel more powerful than my brain?

I could do this; I could pretend to love him. He killed my sister and stole my chance at being married to someone else and having a life I had dreamt of. He took everything from me.

Raj parked the car, and I looked in front of me at a tall, gorgeous stucco building. It was unlike any place I'd ever seen in my life.

"Are you ready for our first date, my beautiful wife?" Raj opened his door and jogged around to mine.

Once opened, I took his hand and looked at my husband in his eyes.

"The first date of many, husband." Pinching my lips together, I looped my arm in his and made my way to the beautiful restaurant.

WE SAT across from each other as a candle flickered between us, surrounded by perfect, red roses.

My eyes wandered wildly as I took it all in. This was the first time I'd been to a restaurant in America. Back in India, the cities all had beautiful restaurants, but in my small village, the food stands were the extent of eating out. Here, the waiters were all wearing bright white tops with black ties, black slacks, and shiny shoes as they bustled around with smiles pinned on their faces.

"Do you know what you want to eat?" Raj was completely unbothered as he read his menu.

"I... I haven't looked at it yet." I lifted the beautiful cream paper and my lips parted in disbelief.

'From this day forward, I'm yours,' was written across

the menu in gold cursive. Glancing up at him, I saw a small smile on his face.

Biting my bottom lip, I tried to suppress the joy I felt, but at the same time, I was repulsed by him. Should he not have been mine since the moment he slid this ring onto my finger?

"Hello, Dr. Rao. It's so good to see you and Mrs. Rao here, again." The waiter's cheeks flushed red as he glanced at me. He was tall, blond, and had bright blue eyes. "Oh, I'm sorry, I thought you were Mrs. Rao." He quickly took a step back, blinking repeatedly.

Raj brushed his fingers against his jawline, looking between the waiter and me. "This is Mrs. Rao, Kai."

Kai's eyes widened as he looked immeasurably uncomfortable. "Hello, Mrs. Rao." He flashed a lopsided smile at me, deepening a dimple in his cheek.

"Gia. My name is Gia." I nodded and smiled back at him.

Clearing his voice, Raj startled us both and I quickly averted my eyes. "Kai, we'd like two orders of the spaghetti carbonara." Raj straightened his back and shoved the menus back at Kai.

"Oh… I wanted to try the alfredo," I mumbled.

"Our fettuccini alfredo is delicious, and my personal favorite." Kai smiled at me yet there was something about the way he smiled that had my stomach tumble with nerves.

"No. She will have what I just ordered," Raj growled aggressively, causing my entire body to tense.

Kai opened his mouth again, but I quickly interjected, "You're right. I can't wait for the spaghetti." Kai looked between us and offered a look of sympathy, but I pretended to not feel it. I pretended everything was fine.

I didn't really enjoy marinara sauce, but I knew better than to correct a man in a public setting. I knew my first time out in the world with my husband would set the stage on how many times he'd ever let me out of the house that became a cage to me.

I kept my eyes on the flickering candle in between us. One of the roses had dipped in, and the petal was burning slowly. I watched as the beautiful red succumbed and shriveled into a black crumble.

"The food here is amazing. I eat here multiple times a week," Raj boasted.

My eyes shot up to his as my lips parted. No wonder we hardly had food at home. He was dining on delicious meals while I starved or eating one of his disgusting meal prepped items. Gritting my teeth together, I balled my hands into fists under the table.

"That's lovely," I forced out, thinking of all the times I had scraped at the butter to lather it onto my dried roti. He didn't even care that his elderly mother was deprived of proper nutrients and meals. I'd make a batch of lentil soup for her, and that was the extent of her heartiest meal.

Raj offered a tight smile back before brushing his finger against the rim of the glass of water repeatedly until it screeched, causing my arms to be splattered with chills.

"This feels awkward, doesn't it? A date, even though we are wed." I looked up at Raj as he continued, "My entire life, I thought I'd escape this… this force that wrapped its claws around me, full of expectations or the repercussions of decisions of those I should have trusted." He paused and my heart began to race. This was the first time Raj was speaking to me in this manner. It was intimate, more than a physical relationship. It felt raw and real. I clung to his words, thirsty for more. If I wanted any chance at living, then I needed to understand this stranger in my life.

"I knew I had to marry a good Indian girl—one who wouldn't think twice about my familial needs and demands. One who would obey and understand her sacrifice was for the greater good of our legacy. I needed an Indian girl to turn into the woman who would carry my son and value how men truly are leaders and pillars of our world. But most of all, I needed a wife who would understand that, while I wish she could be my equal, biologically she'd never be that. She had to be submissive, obedient, and that…

that is how this would work." He pointed his finger between us.

Leaning back in his chair, he opened his palm and slid it into the middle of the table.

I looked down at it, carefully studying the lines, trying to recall my grandmother's words on palmistry.

His life line was long, his heart tapered into two—was that Amara and me? "Take my hand. Tell me you understand that I want to give you the world, but I need you to be the wife I have to have. This shouldn't be abnormal to you. You grew up with women all around you, sacrificing and submitting."

My entire life was this. Being told how I should behave and obsessing over how others would perceive my family if I didn't obey.

"I understand, Raj." I slowly placed my hand into his. Wrapping his fingers around my hand, I stared down at them.

It was in that moment that I knew it was better that his fingers were wrapped around my hand and not my neck.

———

It felt there was more silence than words exchanged as we waited for food. "I'd love to know more about your work," I mustered out, knowing there was something else I would desperately love to know more about.

Raj's eyes lit up. "Well, I'm a doctor, of course, but I am a medical examiner. Basically, I perform autopsies on the departed," he boasted with a satisfied grin, one that crafted chills against my arms the way he said, departed.

"But why the need of a hearse?"

"There are so many people who have their bodies leave the earth with no one there to miss them. Do you know what happens if no one claims a body?"

I lifted my water glass and took a sip before shaking my head.

"The town will simply cremate and dispose of the ashes. In our culture, cremation is a sacred end-of-life ceremony. However, those without loved ones are treated like burning trash. I sometimes handle it all myself. Therefore, a hearse is simply a vehicle suited for the needs of my profession."

Was that truly all that it was? Was Raj simply a dedicated doctor who felt sadness for his patients or the dead?

"Dr. and Mrs. Rao, your meals are ready." Kai broke my train of thought as he rolled the gold cart to our table, full of plates with steam dancing around them. His fitted white dress shirt hugged his body perfectly, as his sleeves were rolled up, displaying tattoos across his veiny forearms. My face flushed as he smiled at me and placed the plates of spaghetti and garlic bread in front of us. "This is on the house." He lifted another plate, one full of thicker noodles covered in a creamy, white sauce.

He placed the plate in front of me and lifted a grater.

I quickly shoveled some of the delicious pasta into my mouth. "Fresh parmesan, anyone?"

Except, I couldn't answer because the way Raj was looking at me and then Kai had my breathing grow still and my hands turn cold.

"We didn't order this." His jaw ticked as he pointed to my plate. Then, with a swift motion, he slammed his hand against the table, causing other restaurant guests to look our way as the porcelain plates and glasses shook.

Kai placed his hands behind his back and looked at me. "I'm sorry, Mrs. Rao, I thought..."

Embarrassment and anger flooded over me, but I knew I couldn't react. He wanted me to, didn't he? Or was this a test? To prove my loyalty to him and our marriage?

"No, it's fine. I'd like to eat it, if that's alright with

my husband, please?" I forced myself to sound genuine and sweet.

The deepened lines on Raj's forehead relaxed as he nodded. "It's fine, yes. I want you to have anything you want."

Glancing up at Kai, as Raj looked down to spiral spaghetti on his fork, I mouthed, 'Thank you.' The light in Kai's blue eyes twinkled as he pursed his lips and winked at me.

Immediately looking at my plate, I waited for him to retreat before lifting my fork as my stomach fluttered and my heart raced.

Taking another bite of the fettuccini alfredo, I moaned. It was phenomenal.

But it wasn't just that. It was the fact that another man knew how to make me happier than my husband, that he cared to let me decide. It was the fact that I knew I couldn't live like this forever. I had to escape; I had to figure out everything I could about the man sitting across from me and make sure my sister's soul was at peace, but after that I'd escape. I had to.

After eating our meals in silence, Kai came back with a chocolate cake stacked high on a plate and placed it between us.

"Congrats on your new marriage, Dr. and Mrs. Rao." He didn't smile, he simply laid the plate and silverware down. Raj looked pleased and immediately dug in with his fork. Before Kai left, his hand knocked my napkin onto the floor, but it didn't seem accidental. Flustered, he reached down and lifted it up.

"I'm so sorry, Mrs. Rao. Here's a clean napkin. He tugged out the folded cloth and carefully handed it to me."

Raj glanced at us once. "Bring us another one of these to go," he ordered rudely. Kai immediately nodded, but before leaving us, he widened his eyes at my napkin.

Looking down at it, I placed it in my lap, and he cleared his throat, blinking repeatedly and staring at it.

What the hell is he doing?

"Eat the cake." Raj slid a fork to me as Kai quickly turned away. Carefully unfolding my napkin, I saw it.

A small piece of paper peeked out. "Gia, give me your napkin. The damn waiter took it with my plate." Lifting my eyes to my husband, I couldn't think straight. I slid the paper out and clung to it in one hand. I didn't have a pocket or purse. Why clothing companies ever thought men needed pockets more than women would forever boggle my mind. After all, we have so much to carry, including their baggage.

"Napkin. Now." Slanting my eyes at him, I bit my tongue. So much for a date night. After I handed my napkin to him, I looked over my shoulder. "I'm going to the restroom."

Standing, I couldn't believe I had simply stated what I was going to do versus asking. All evening, I realized, that's what Raj had done. He told me what to do, what to eat, how to behave. I always asked. My entire life was an ask.

Once in the beautiful marble and gold restroom—I would have otherwise paused and relished in—I unfolded the note and looked at the small words.

It was a phone number and a message.

Just in case you don't want the spaghetti and need take-out.

My chest rose and fell rapidly as I looked up at the girl in the reflection and breathed out. He knew. He knew I was in trouble with Raj. Walking into a bathroom stall, I lifted my dress and slid the note into the elastic of my panties. Just as I was tugging my dress down, the door flung open.

I gasped, but it wasn't a stranger…

It was Raj.

His eyes filled with anger as tinges of red splattered into the whites. "What are you doing? This is the ladies' bathroom." I shoved past him quickly as my stomach flipped.

"I thought he…"

Washing my hands, I looked into the mirror and saw Raj sulking.

"You thought he what?" My eyebrows knitted

together as I reached for the paper towel and dried my hands before turning back to my husband.

"Kai... the waiter. I thought he followed you in here. I couldn't bear to think of another man with you, Gia." He brushed his hands through his hair.

I became winded, even though I was just standing there. Raj Rao, my husband, was jealous.

I had him right where I needed him to be.

Or so I thought...

**CHAPTER
EIGHTEEN**

I DIDN'T WANT to leave the city. It was beautiful and bright, and even when the darkness seeped into the sky, all the tall buildings and homes we passed were lit up. It was such a stark contrast from where we were, isolated in a crumbling home by the ocean with tormented souls lurking. I felt like an actual human for the first time since coming to this new country. *The land of the free...* I thought and scoffed. I had never been more confined and stripped of my rights than here. I grew up dreaming of America—so many of us did. We'd see the magazines with gorgeous celebrities, homes, and lifestyles. We'd hear the rare story of the boy or girl from our village getting a work visa or student visa and falling in love with this glorified unknown land.

As soon as the plane landed, I remember thinking

how strikingly beautiful it all was. I remember thinking how everyone seemed to have a purpose here and a voice.

But most of all, I remember thinking I'd be able to have that, too.

I watched as the lights danced past through the window. The depraved odor of the hearse suffocated me as I tried to focus on something, anything else.

"I'm sorry about the restroom incident. I… I hope it didn't ruin our date." Raj gripped the worn leather steering wheel as vulnerability seeped into his words.

"Raj, I know that we hardly know each other. I knew the circumstance of our wedding was based on grief, pain, and loss, but I am your wife. I hope you know I would never disrespect the institution of marriage or you."

His lips tipped upward, and I quickly looked back out the window, knowing that as soon as the lights vanished, so did this false impression of our marriage.

The car tires crunched against the gravel as we drove on the winding road back up to the estate. It had so much potential. It was a massive residence, secluded, with views of the ocean. Much like my marriage, the idea of it was a dream, but the reality of it was a nightmare.

As soon as I opened the door, I drank in the fresh air. The smell of death and rot clung to my skin. "Does the smell of the car not bother you?" I asked Raj as we walked side-by-side into the house.

Jamming the old, gold key into the doorknob, Raj waved me inside first. Looking behind me, his eyes widened and he shook his head slowly.

My body tensed as a cold gust caused the door to slam open completely.

"Raj?" I looked over my shoulder.

He quickly feigned a smile and shut the door behind us. "The smell of the car doesn't bother me. The odor is not emitting from the deceased I've had to transport, but rather, from formaldehyde. As a man of science, this is a scent I'm more accustomed to than any artificial fragrance candle or whatnot," Raj said as he locked the door. There wasn't just one lock, there were four, which always confused me, considering most of what I feared wasn't outside of this house, but rather in it.

"It's late, Gia. I'm going to bathe you, and then we can get into bed together."

I froze in the foyer. "You're going to give me a bath?" I let out a forced laugh, attempting to mask the confusion I felt.

"Yes, you are filthy from being in the city. From being around that man who was staring at you, and…" Raj shuddered as he closed his eyes.

"What man?"

"The waiter."

I erupted into laughter. "Raj, you must be joking. How am I filthy because our waiter at a restaurant spoke to me? About food, nonetheless." I continued to laugh as Raj and I stood under the dusty, yet grand chandelier that caught light in each crystal.

"Get in the tub, Gia." Raj's voice was eerily low. But I couldn't take him seriously. How could I? I finally, after months, leave these four walls on a romantic date night, and we come home with him assuming the waiter has caused me to become filthy?

I shook my head and covered my mouth because I couldn't stop giggling. But then his facial expression changed.

He lifted his hand and slapped me. The sound of his palm and my soft flesh clapping together with impact as my head abruptly turned echoed around us.

My lips parted, but I didn't make a sound. I was in disbelief, shock. But most of all, regret.

I was full of regret that my husband slapped me, and I blamed myself completely.

I knew better than to push him enough to begin what I knew would be an endless circle of now physical abuse.

The most difficult part in hurting someone physically is the very first time. Just like many things in life, we become comfortable, we become confident.

Lifting my hand to my pulsing cheek, I looked down and clamped my lips together. Tears brimmed my eyes as I prayed he couldn't see how my body trembled.

He sighed and took a step closer, which only caused me to stumble back in fear as I winced.

"Amara, my darling." Raj leaned in and wrapped his arms around me. "I'm so sorry. I didn't mean to, my love. I'm sorry. I'm sorry," he repeated over and over again, but it just began to blur together.

My mind was no longer clouded with his words and forged apologies, but rather, if he slapped me so easily—all because a male waiter spoke to me—then how many times must he have hurt my sister? How many times over the course of desperation for a son did he beat her?

"I'm Gia," I cried, but he didn't care. I was whoever he wanted me to be—much like the entirety of my life.

This silly game I was playing, thinking I could be a detective, take this man down, and solve what really happened to my sister was imprudent, but most of all, it was deadly.

How stupid could I have been to think I could single-handedly solve my sister's death, escape this man, and start a life worth living?

"Please go to the bath. I don't want to hurt you. I won't hurt you." Raj released me and moved out of my way. Brushing the tears from my face, I walked up the stairs, gripping the banister, wishing I could rip it off and stab him to death.

Before walking to our bedroom, I turned toward Mami's room. Poor lady had been here all evening, alone, because her psychotic son wouldn't hire assistance. Granted, why would he? I was the help.

Opening her door slowly, the creaking had me grimacing. "Mami…" I whispered. A small candle flickered on top of her dresser. Did Raj light it? The candle wax pooled by the tarnished holder.

I crept toward her bedside and looked at the mostly empty plate. Relieved that she had eaten something, I leaned in and brushed away the hair sticking to her forehead. She needed proper medical care, a caretaker, and something more than this small room with no interaction. No one sent the elderly to retirement homes or care centers in India; it was our duty to care for them the way they cared for us. But I wasn't prepared to take this level of care of someone.

"Goodnight, Mami," I whispered as I slowly pulled away, except her hand shot up and grabbed my hair. Dragging my head down to her face, the tips of our noses touched and she smiled. Her teeth were mostly missing, while her breath reeked of rotting food.

My eyes widened as she whispered, "There is nothing good that comes from the night here, silly little girl." Laughing wickedly before choking on her saliva and coughing, I let out of a cry.

"Mami!"

She began growling in my face and speaking in a language I didn't understand.

My scalp ached as she tugged my hair harder. Reaching down to her hands, I plucked her fingers off and tugged away. Racing out of her room, I began crying as the doors I ran past began slamming shut one by one.

"Raj!" I screamed. No answer.

I wanted to die.

AS SOON AS I walked into our bedroom, I heard the water running in the bathroom. My stomach twisted into knots. I quickly hid the note from Kai as tears filled my eyes.

He was humming an unfamiliar song as I dragged my feet across the cold wood floors. "Come to me, my beloved," he called out. My heart was pounding as I wiped my tears.

Walking toward the window, I tugged the curtains away from it, feeling numb.

I could jump out and die against the boulders and then the ocean could carry me away into its dark depths.

No one would miss me, no one would think twice. I could be free.

But as soon as I tucked the curtains away, nausea crept into my stomach.

There were metal bars on the windows. I knew for a fact they hadn't been there before. What changed? Worse of all, what was going to change enough for him to add bars to the windows? What was going to change so much that he'd need to cage me in even more?

I would have noticed if someone had come here to put them in. I would have noticed if a lifeline was right in front of my face without Raj present.

Except suddenly, realization poured over me. Raj took me on a date so we'd be out of the house. "Gia," he sang out, his voice echoing in the large but decaying bathroom.

If he had bars installed on the windows, what else did he add to the house? Forcing myself to make my way to the bathroom, I stood at the doorframe.

He was kneeling by the claw-tub that I assume was once white but now yellowed. The lights were off, but multiple candles flickered all around.

Without turning to look at me, he dragged his fingers into the water.

"It's perfectly warm. Undress now."

He was my husband. He had seen me naked and had me in bed with him. But this seemed far more inti-mate. This seemed like something a couple in love did.

Raj didn't love me; he was showing me his control over me. Something he had without a sliver of doubt.

I took my clothes off and immediately covered myself with my arms. Swallowing the lump in my throat, I climbed into the tub with my eyes closed, yet I could still feel Raj's heavy gaze on me.

Dipping my toes in and sliding into the tub, I exhaled. The water was too hot while the room was too frigid. Opening my eyes, I looked at the rose petals sitting on already subsided bubbles and sprinkles of something all over it that looked like pepper or cinnamon.

Staring straight ahead but clearly seeing him through my peripheral, he lifted a small sponge and saturated it with soap.

"I need you to do something for me tonight, wife," he rasped as he began cleansing my arm. I hated how the bubbles had melted away and my body was on full display through the water full of useless suds.

Gritting my teeth, fear coursed through my veins. His voice dropped even lower. "There will be repercussions if you don't."

"What is it?" My voice broke as I slowly turned to look at him.

"I need you to be my Amara tonight." His deep brown eyes stayed on mine. His lips cut downward as if his outlandish statement had pained him.

The air shook as it left my lips.

"I miss her. She… brought light to this otherwise dark hole I find my life to be. I feel her visiting me sometimes. I know she's here; I know she's embedded into these walls. I can't let her go. I won't…" Raj rushed out while rubbing the loofah against my skin.

"I'm assuming I bring darkness?" I flicked my eyes at him. I didn't understand why envy panged me. Was I jealous that my husband was still in love with his first wife, or was I jealous that my husband was still in love with my now-dead sister?

"What would it take for you to love me the way you loved her?" I looked into his deep, dark chocolate eyes.

Raj sighed as he straightened his shoulders. "Be her. Please just be her. She was perfect except for…"

"Except for what?" I hated the way the humidity of the heat from the tub radiated upward and made my hair cling to the nape of my neck. I hated how he was cleaning me, and how I never felt dirtier in my life.

"She died."

Blinking slowly, I didn't know what to feel. This man really did love her. Why would he ever hurt her?

"I'll let you finish your bath in solitude and after, I request that you join me in bed. I have needs. As your husband, I shouldn't feel as if I'm asking a lot to be…" He paused, only making the moment even more uncomfortable. "If you don't start being my wife, then I'll send you back to your parents... one way or another. I will take everything from them."

In my time here, I knew I had pushed limits. I had defied Raj, and I had been a mostly terrible wife. But with that one statement, reality hit me harder than the way I dreamed of my body hitting the rocks below.

If I chose to continue to try to defy him, he'd take me home—and I was certain it would be in an urn.

I couldn't do that to my parents. I couldn't take their daughters and their livelihood away. They didn't have a son to take care of them. Even though Mami was rotting away, she still was in a warm home. She had two people to hear her if she needed anything. My parents didn't have that—they'd never have that. What would happen when one of them died?

At least they'd have the money from their farm, and I could convince Raj to help them. It was my job to take care of my parents.

And my husband.

Had I gone so far down a hole of insanity that I was simply crafting stories to make myself have an excuse as to why this life was one I never wanted?

Looking at the water, I opened the drain and ran the tap.

Rinsing my body off, I knew that as soon as the tub emptied, so had my time.

I had to be whoever he wanted me to be. Especially to get what I wanted.

I STOOD in front of the fogged mirror, gliding my hand across the steam with my eyes closed. I could do it. I could. Opening them slowly, I saw her.

Amara.

A smile grew on my face. I took the used lipstick that was hers and plastered it over my pout, then ran my hands through my unruly hair.

Loosening the strap of my robe, I exhaled feeling the fear leave my body. Gia was scared; Gia looked for every single opportunity to run from the life chosen for her. But Amara loved Raj. Amara loved being a submissive, good bride.

Amara wasn't scared.

I opened the door and walked into the bedroom where Raj was laying in the bed. His chest was bare, and the rest of his body was covered by the plush blanket.

His eyes lit up as he lifted his body against his forearm. "Amara, my beloved." The shift in his tone pained me. He was in love with her.

I wanted to feel it. I wanted to feel what my sister must have felt from this man.

"Hello, husband," I forced out, ignoring the awkwardness.

His lips curved into a genuine smile, full of joy and pride. "I know how much you wanted to be a mother, Amu," he crooned as I cringed at the nickname. "We will be a family, I promise you. Just give me a son. Your only flaw, my love, was not being able to give me a son."

The candles Raj had lit around the room began to flicker wildly as a blanket of cold air seemingly wrapped itself around me. A howl and echo radiated in the room causing us to both freeze in fear.

"Raj…" I whispered with my voice raspy.

I could hear a baby crying.

"Raj!" His eyes were rolling as he laid flat into the bed.

My heart pounded as I ran to the bed and pulled the blanket over my body.

Minutes passed as the noises blended together. I clung to the blanket as Raj began to peel it off of me.

"Amara, don't be scared. Don't be. You know what this house is made of. I told you that the pain it holds within its walls will disappear as soon as we bring a son into it. You must..."

He reached down and cradled my face before brushing his lips against mine. As soon as he did, the candles flickered out completely.

We are conditioned to be scared of the dark, but in this moment, I was grateful. I could easily be Amara and believe it myself because Gia was too scared.

———

Raj's arm was flung over my body as I rested my head on the pillow and listened. It wasn't his snoring that was keeping me up, it was the way I could hear an inexplicable clanking sound. The vent right by my side of the bed wasn't blowing air out, but the noise ricocheted from it every single night. Suddenly, I thought about how Mami was huddled over the vent, singing a song.

I couldn't piece it all together. My brain felt fuzzy, and the sleep deprivation was finally taking its toll on me.

Closing my eyes, I let myself fall deeper into the

darkness. I felt my body tumble down a dark tunnel, yet I felt lighter, freer. Maybe because as I fell asleep, I told myself I was Amara and Amara didn't care about peculiar noises or flickering lights. She wasn't scared, not anymore.

And for the first time as I felt warm and cozy which was a nice relief from how cold I normally felt.

———

I stood over the bubbling pot of chai. Raj had finally bought fresh ginger, cardamom, and cinnamon.

"Mmm, smells good." He sounded happy and not sinister like he usually did. Wrapping his arms around my waist, I realized I was holding my breath.

"Thank you for bringing these fresh ingredients," I said quietly. He released his hold around me and waltzed through the kitchen with his arms out as he sang an old Bollywood song. My lips parted in shock as he danced and sang wildly.

A sizzle cracked through the moment, and I flung back around to the stove.

"Oh my." I cut the gas off and quickly removed the pot. "I'll clean it, I will." Fear coursed through me, thinking Raj would become upset and I'd see the side of him that terrified me to my core.

He grabbed my arm and turned me around. The

lines between his brows had deepened but then he opened his mouth and belted out another song while moving my body around the kitchen and dancing with me excitedly.

My gown floated behind me as I clung to his hands and couldn't help but savor this moment.

Laughing loudly, Raj dipped me before kissing my forehead. "Amara, I love you."

The smile on my face froze in place before melting off. Raj lifted me back up, then grabbed a travel thermos from the half-broken shelf.

Pouring the chai through a strainer, he fastened the lid and quickly grabbed his keys and wallet.

But just before he left, he turned. He tossed his head back and whispered something under his breath. I watched him disappear down the hall. I shuddered as he started to yell and slam things, not daring to even look around.

Moments later, he came back into the kitchen with something in his hands. His face was lit up with excitement. It was a freezer bag with something in an unsettling red tinged with brown. Swallowing the lump in my throat, I looked at him.

"What is that?" I whispered and leaned in closer as

he swiftly turned around grabbing utensils and a stained to-go dish.

Blinking, I slapped my hand across my mouth as I was certain hair was tangled into whatever the food was.

"It's my favorite kind of meat." Raj said calmly as he threw everything into a container.

My lips parted but no words came out.

"Dead women." He smirked. I could feel the blood drain from my face.

He brushed his hands down my face before wrapping his hand around my neck and pushing me backwards. Tightening his grip, he began leaning in.

Blowing a breath of air into my face, he smiled. "You'd be the most delicious. But unfortunately, you've still got a heartbeat."

"Raj," I choked out as tears dripped down my face and my breathing became erratic.

Loosening his grip, he began laughing wildly before suddenly stopping.

"Take a joke, my love." Shutting the door behind him, I watched the ugly, pale yellow curtain tremor. It had small butterflies on it, and I could hear her voice. I don't think I'd ever paid close enough attention to it before.

"Run, run, my little butterfly." I spun around, swearing I could hear her voice.

Had she known all along that I was going to be here? Had she set me up?

Running to the door, I screamed and ripped the curtain off violently, angrily ripping it to shreds with my bare hands before the jingle.

Mami. She was ringing the damn bell.

Slamming the shreds of the curtain into the trash, I grabbed a packet of crackers and a pitcher of water and stormed up the stairs. Fear was surging through my body. I began gagging as I froze in front of Mami's door. Was my husband eating dead women for lunch?

MAMI WAS LYING in the bed with her arm hanging off and snoring loudly. Furrowing my brows, I looked at her bedside table where the bell was no longer sitting. Spinning around the room, I saw it on the small, cluttered dresser.

"Mami..." My voice crackled. She didn't even flinch, but the curtains began to sway and when I squinted, I could see an outline of a shadow.

Slowing my breath, I put one foot in front of the other and gradually made my way over. My teeth were gritting together as my heart raced, and I reached my hand out to the curtain.

"Amu," she rasped, causing me to jerk around and flinging my arm across my chest.

Glancing over my shoulder, the shadow was gone.

The wood floors creaked as my feet dragged against them.

"Amu," Mami whined, the lines across her forehead deepening as her eyes clenched shut.

I was going to correct her, but then my silence rewarded me. "Amu, did you take the prenatal?" Mami said so clearly, I couldn't believe it was her.

I felt my chest tighten with the realization that all the answers to my questions were finally right in front of me.

"Yes, Mami. What else do you think I should do?" I swallowed the lump in my throat.

"Do you have another photo for me?" Mami kept her eyes closed, but a small smile grew on her face.

A photo? Brushing my hand across my stomach, I felt as if my breathing was restricted.

"No. Not yet," I mustered out. Mami nodded and lifted her hand, sticking her pointer finger out. I followed the direction she was pointing toward; it was her dresser.

"Your bell? Mami, how did your bell move?" I made my way toward it, but she began coughing.

Between gasps for air, she said, "No. Photo."

I looked at the gold-brushed metal box sitting by the bell. Opening it carefully, I was taken aback that it was actually a music box. A small ballerina began twirling to morose music.

There were small trinkets, broken gold chains, random earrings, and shards of paper with scribbles.

Fingering through the miscellaneous items, I got to the bottom, which were faded, wallet-sized photos.

"Amu, bring it." Mami coughed out.

What was I looking for?

As soon as she said those words, I lifted a folded, thinner piece of paper. Flipping it over, my lips parted in shock.

Amara Rao. My sister's name and birth date were printed at the top right of the black-and-white image.

It was an ultrasound image. Gestational period: thirty-eight weeks, one day.

My sister was pregnant, and she was full-term.

I was staring at an image of my niece or nephew.

"Amu!" Mami screeched.

I ran over to her and handed her the photo.

Slowly opening her eyes, her entire face lit up.

Brushing her fingers against the image, tears rolled down her cheeks.

"Mami, where is my baby?" I couldn't believe the words I was saying.

Where is my sister?

"I know you miss baby, Amu. Baby died. Baby died, Amu." Mami hysterically sobbed while clutching the ultrasound photo to her chest.

Tears filled my eyes as I thought of the child I never

got to meet. A baby who was a part of me. My sister…
my older, beautiful, kind-hearted sister had a baby.
Here. In this hell, she had a sliver of peace and hope.

"How?" I cried out.

Mami shook her head and looked at me through
her wet eyes, clouded by cataracts.

"Who are you?" she shrieked, then fell back into
her pillow and began screaming.

Grabbing the photos from her jewelry box, I
slammed it shut and ran out.

———

Sitting on the floor of the room I first lived in, I stared
at the stack of images. There was one of a family. A
pregnant woman, a man, and a little boy.

The small scar that ran across the little boy's cheek
matched the one on Raj's face. The pregnant woman
had to be Mami. She looked completely different—
young and beautiful, with thick lips and long lashes. It
saddened me to think of this woman becoming…
Looking up at the door, I thought of the deteriorating
woman right down the hall.

The man in the photo looked so much like Raj now.
How could Raj never have mentioned siblings?

Where did they live?

Moving to the next photo, I lifted it up. "Amara," I

gasped. It was a photo of my sister laughing in the kitchen.

She looked happy.

She was happy.

She was happy here.

Placing the photos down, I kept going through the stack.

Photos of Amara and Raj, old black-and-white images, and then one last photo that shattered me.

Raj cradling a small baby.

I needed to find the baby.

I MADE ROTI, lentil soup, and rice while being void of any emotion. I wondered if Raj was eating out at some nice restaurant as I ate the same thing every night, and often every afternoon.

But then the kitchen door creaked open and heavy footsteps stomped in.

"There she is," he boasted. I turned and looked at my husband, who was donning a huge grin and holding a bouquet of red roses in his arms.

"Here you are," he said, handing them to me before he gripped my face and planted a kiss on my cheek.

Clearing my throat, I took them from him and thought better that he is handing them to me and not laying them on my rotting body.

"Did you eat?" I asked as I lifted my plate.

He took it from me and shook his head. "I want to eat with my wife."

Maybe a good wife would feel elated that her husband came home to have dinner with her or that he brought roses. Maybe a good wife would feel grateful she didn't have to have a "real" job and could go about her day, albeit in four walls, but I wasn't a good wife. No, I wanted to know why the man I called my husband failed to mention the fact that he was a father...

A father to my sister's child.

But I knew for a fact I couldn't let Raj know that I knew. If he did something to both of them, then I knew he wouldn't hesitate to do something to me.

Making a second plate for myself, I followed Raj to the oversized formal table. He was lighting the candlesticks and waved for me to sit down. Instead of the seat next to him, I sank into the chair at the opposite end.

"This is delicious, Amara. A nice change to my usual." He smiled as he shoveled food into his mouth. "How was your day?" A speck of rice fell from his lips.

I clenched my fist and watched him.

"Amara?"

The candlesticks shook as I slammed my fist against the table. "Do. Not. Call. Me. That," I seethed with rage fuming through my body.

Raj didn't react. Instead, he carefully placed his

spoon down, leaned back in the chair, and stared at me. "I'm sorry. Did I hear a woman raise her voice at me?" He mockingly cupped his ear and looked around.

The fury-fueled confidence seemingly withered away like sand in an hourglass.

"Did I hear a woman, who I single-handedly saved from a fucking village and poverty, attempt to tell me what to do?"

Raj stood slowly and walked to me.

"I saved your family from the trenches of rotting in some makeshift house and dying from starvation." He scoffed. Reaching out, he grabbed my arm violently.

"Raj!" I exclaimed with shock.

"What would you prefer I call you?" He dragged me with both hands to the library and threw me onto the velvet couch.

"Gia," I whimpered, keeping my eyes low but seeing his hand lift in the air through my peripherals. "I want to be Gia."

His hand relaxed as I clutched the pillow and exhaled.

Sinking down on his knees, he brushed my hair from my face. "Gia..."

"Let's go to bed." He kissed my forehead and helped me up from the couch. As I walked past the foggy mirror, I saw a reflection that had my entire body grow cold.

It was my face, but I was pale. There were dark bags under my eyes and my hair was half gone. Leaning closer, I parted my lips and screamed.

Maggots were crawling out of my mouth. Flinging around, I sprinted and ran straight into Raj.

He steadied me, tilting my head up with his index finger. "Dakini. She's here." His eyes filled with sadness as if he knew what I had just seen, making it even more terrifying knowing that it wasn't just me. It wasn't just me seeing things or hearing things. What kind of life was I living where being mentally ill would have been the better option.

"I don't understand…" I whimpered as I followed behind him.

Raj shrugged and clutched the wooden banister before looking at the dusty, antique chandelier above that began to sway, causing the crystals to chime.

"If you'd give me a son, then you'd know the curse would end." Although I grew up in a culture, family, and community that emphasized a supernatural aspect with spirits, ghosts, and black magic, I never thought I believed in it. But I suppose you can't believe in something that you've never experienced. We blindly follow religious beliefs and traditions without a second thought. What did a son have to do with a curse in this house? Most of all, who was Dakini, and how did Raj not see that it was my sister's unsettled soul lurking in these tormented walls?

I begrudgingly crawled into bed with Raj and waited for the annoying putter of his snoring to echo. As I waited, there it was—the clanking. Looking around, I stared at the air vent. Sliding out of bed, I listened carefully as the musty air blew through.

Tap, tap, tap.

Shaking my head, I stood and slowly left the bedroom. Going down the steps, I winced at the creaking of the floorboards. The house was silent and completely dark. Flipping the switch on in the library, for some reason, it didn't work. Gritting my teeth, I put my hands out and patted around for the kitchen until I tugged open a drawer, knowing candlesticks and matches were always kept there.

Slicing the match against the matchbox, I watched the flame sizzle before lighting the candle and walking back to the library. I paused with each step I took because I felt a shadow larger than my own laying over me.

"Amara?" I whispered, her name shaking between my lips.

Silence.

I held the candle up and looked at the rows and rows of books. There had to be answers. Brushing my fingers against the spines, I read them until I reached a bookshelf with titles I'd never heard of. Some were scribbled out in Hindi, with worn leather binding and discoloration.

Padding my finger across them, I saw one turned the wrong way and dug it out from the tight space.

Laying it into my palms, I squinted at the embossed gold title on the bumpy black leather cover.

The title translated to *Indian Mythology: Demons and spirits*. The fiery wax of the candle dripped onto my fingers, and I quickly placed it down on the end table. Sinking down in the wing-back chair, I opened it and flipped to one of the pages that had been marked with a tab.

Images of gods and goddesses with multiple heads, mouths hung open and sharp teeth, splattered across the pages, while words in Sanskrit—the holy language of India—were scribbled out. I flipped to the second tab and felt my fingers burn as a note toppled out. Lifting it up, I held it beside the words on the page. *Dakini.* A black and white image of a woman dangling male heads stared back at me.

Someone had written out a translation on the note.

Dakini is a woman who dies during childbirth or preg-nancy and comes back as a spirit to haunt, kill, and harm the man responsible for her pain. She can alter reality.

My heart raced as my mouth grew dry.

Dakini's wrath is stopped when she saves her child and the one she loves.

The candle began flickering wildly as cold air flooded through the library window.

I thought it was the wind howling, but when I stood and walked to the window, I could see the waves grow bigger and swore it was a woman's voice. A woman in despair.

Did my sister become some possessed, demonic spirit? Was this why Raj wanted a son? So, he could sacrifice my child to…

My dead sister?

Shaking my head, I shuddered. He was mentally ill. I wouldn't believe this. No. My sister would never want me to go through this. She'd never haunt or hurt me. If she knew I was married to her husband, then she'd know for sure it was out of obligation not desire.

The butterfly drawn in the shower steam, the words written in blood, and the shadows lurking? That… that could be my imagination. I hadn't been sleeping much, and I barely ate. My body was deteriorating each day. Anyone could go crazy in these circumstances.

Shutting the book, I refused to believe in ancient superstitions. I refused to be a pawn in my husband's psychosis.

Standing, I slammed it back into its spot before closing the window and grabbing what was left of the candlestick. I looked around the house. It was truly magnificent. With the right residents, money, and care, it would be a beautiful home to fill with family and memories. I wondered what it had looked like before it went to hell.

Wandering the halls, I supposed I had never truly toured the entirety of it. Maybe it was because I didn't really care to since I always wanted to leave it. There was no desire to become attached to something I was constantly trying to escape from.

I turned the corner and kept going down the hall to a closed door. Gripping the steel knob, I turned it and, to my surprise, it opened.

Looking over my shoulder and down at the candle, I exhaled and walked in. Flipping the switch, the light was still out. It looked like a storage room, cluttered with random junk and boxes.

The stench of rotting, dust, and moisture burned my eyes and clogged my throat. Coughing and covering my face with one hand, I froze as a sound echoed.

It was the clanking.

Stilling my breathing, I walked to a wall covered with shelves. Photo albums covered in a thick layer of dust, medical textbooks—I guess he really was a doctor —and miscellaneous items were crammed together.

The clanking grew louder as I pressed my ear

against a sliver of the wall that hadn't been covered. I couldn't tell without proper lighting and moving the shelves if there was a door. What was behind this wall?

But just as I began trying to drag the first shelf away from it, the candle's flame burnt out.

And there was nothing more terrifying than being in the dark, not knowing what was lurking right by you.

"Hello?" I rasped.

Silence.

I walked backwards slowly and immediately I felt a hand on my back. My breathing hitched as I slammed my lips together.

"Raj?"

Fingernails dragged against my back as my spine straightened. And in that moment, I knew, it wasn't Raj.

It was Dakini. Looking down at my nails, I shuddered. They needed to be cut.

TWENTY-THREE

I LAID IN BED, staring up at the ceiling, knowing Raj's alarm would be going off at any moment. I'd be expected to make him breakfast and smile as if I didn't just discover what could be a secret lair, along with haunted books about spirits and sacrificing my first-born. The flesh on my back burned. Whatever, whoever that was…cut through my skin with their nails and I had no one to tell. No one to talk to. I felt hopeless and fearful to even let my foot hang off the bed or use the bathroom.

I had to leave. This was the final straw. There was no rationalizing with Raj. I'd never find out what happened to my sister or help her soul rest. I wouldn't be able to change anything, and something I was coming to realize was that change was inevitable only for those who welcomed it.

This house would kill me.

I didn't have credit cards, cash, or a phone. How would I even run away in a country I knew nothing about or had no one to even rely on?

How could I cross an entire ocean to go to a home that would never open its door to me?

People are quick to judge. Why didn't she just leave? Why did she stay? She could have left. But the magnitude of it all is terrifying. I'd starve or freeze to death, and as for shelters? Raj had warned me about them. But maybe I could take the risk and find a shelter for women and see if they could at least help me figure out a way to get back to India.

But where would I go in India? My parents would be ruined and, on the streets, if I left Raj because he'd pull all funding and support of their farm away. Society would crush them with their judgmental claws since one daughter had died and the other ran away from her perfect doctor husband.

Sweat beads lined my hairline as stress pooled in my abdomen. But the buzzing of Raj's alarm startled me and I slammed my eyes shut. Raj always got up on the first buzz. He'd slide out of bed, take a long shower, trim his beard, and put on a nice outfit. He didn't look like he lived in this house. I was positive no one at the supposed hospital he worked at would have guessed he lived in a rotting estate by the water plagued with death.

I sat up and got out of bed as soon as I heard the shower turn on. Hurrying downstairs, I began preparing his chai and toast. My stomach was growling as I spread the butter, and I peeked around the wall to see the door at the end of the hallway. I knew what I'd do today. I had to figure out where that noise was coming from, and what was behind the wall.

Then, I'd call my parents and beg them to send me a plane ticket. Once in my own country, I'd figure it out. I had friends I could stay with. I had…

The bell jingled. Mami. She was up, too. Who would take care of her when I left? She was in such terrible shape when I got here. I knew my sister must have taken care of her to the best of her ability—that was who Amara was, a caretaker. I didn't allow myself to think of the ultrasound photos. I didn't allow myself to picture my laughing, beautiful sister cradling a baby belly. I couldn't do it without nausea sliding into my esophagus.

Raj entered the kitchen as I was putting things on a tray for Mami. "Good morning, my love." He smiled at me.

I forced a grin out and quickly turned to the tray.

"I was thinking we could go on a little vacation," Raj said calmly.

Gripping the wooden handles, I turned slowly to look at him.

He walked closer to me. "We never took a honeymoon." Tilting my chin up, he brushed his lips across mine.

I could feel my cheeks grow warm at this small, completely normal sign of affection.

Nodding, I said, "I'd love that."

I could get out of this house. I could find help.

He smiled before looking down at the tray in my hands. "Is that for Mami?" Lifting the toast off the plate, he took a bite before placing it back down.

"Don't worry, my love. She won't be a burden on us much longer. We are so close…" His words came out icy.

"What do you mean? Is she ill?" I felt frantic and guilty. I knew I should have been doing a better job of caring for her. It was my responsibility. *She* was my responsibility.

"Of course, she's ill. She is an elderly, paralyzed woman who hardly eats or moves. What kind of life is that? As a physician, I swore to never see someone in pain and not fix it. So, by the end of the week, I'll fix it, and then we will go on our honeymoon. The last thing I need is to come home to a decomposing body and the odor rampaging through our home."

My eyes widened as Raj spoke, and I shook my head. "What do you mean you'll fix *it*?" How could he speak about his mother this way?

A sinister smirk grew across his face as he tugged something out of his wallet and handed it over to me. "Here, I want you to go buy new clothes and whatever beauty products you'd like to make yourself look… well, attractive. We are going to change things around here, starting with our honeymoon."

I was in disbelief as I took the credit card while completely numb to the insults he had said with ease. "I don't have a car," I whispered. "I'll drop you off in town. I have a shorter day at work today, so I will pick you back up. All the stores you'd be interested in are in walking distance from one another."

My heart ached for the fact that, in any other lifetime, this moment would be considered swoon-worthy. But for me, this wasn't a way to admire my husband more; it was a way to seek help for not just me but for Mami, too. Looking up at the ceiling, I cleared my throat. "What did you mean about…"

. . .

"Your curiosity is going to get you into trouble. She is my mother; she has told me her wishes, and I will abide by them. On Friday, I will inject my mother with a drug that will help her sleep for eternity. We will do a ceremony and say our goodbyes. I know we will meet again in another lifetime. She will always be my mother, and as for you, my bride, we promised seven lifetimes together."

"Run upstairs and give Mami her food, and then come back down changed. I don't want to be late to see my patients and keep them waiting.

"Aren't your patients all dead?" I asked as I walked away.

Raj crossed his arms and nodded. "The dead are more restless than the living. They need me to listen to their stories. They need me to listen to their final wishes. They need me to hold them."

My body froze as I gripped the banister and looked down at him. A small smile grew on his face.

"Go on, my love. We must depart soon."

THE CAR RIDE into town was quicker than I realized. If I ever ran away, I could get straight into town by foot. Sure, it may take me an hour to figure my way out, but I tried to memorize landmarks and watch the clock.

"For our honeymoon, I was thinking I could take you to New York City." Raj looked over at me.

I had always dreamt of visiting New York. In my mind, it was the definition of America. But I knew I wouldn't see it. I had one week to save Mami and figure out a way to leave.

"That sounds great." I feigned a smile as Raj stopped in front of a boutique.

"Have fun. I'll pick you up in a few hours. Grab some food out here, too. There are tons of restaurants and places to eat."

Sliding out of the car, I couldn't help but feel happiness. I guess ending off this chapter of my life with a shopping spree wouldn't be such a bad idea. I knew I needed to buy things I could pack easily and tie me over to wherever I went to next.

"I love you. Have fun!" My mouth dropped as I turned back as I looked at my husband in shock.

Rolling up the window, he sped off as I stood there in the middle of street I had never been to with a credit card in my hand and worn clothes on my back.

He loved me?

Cars began honking, and I quickly stepped onto the sidewalk. I looked around at all the stores. Well-dressed, beautiful people were sipping coffee with their arms linked. Everyone looked happy. The excited chatter, the scent of delicious food, the stunning shops.

This was living.

They were living.

I walked into the boutique and was in awe of the gorgeous dresses, skirts, high-fashion jewelry, purses, and shoes. I loved clothes and all things fashion, but never in my life had the means to enjoy it. Lifting up a gorgeous, red silk dress, I admired the shine of it.

"Mrs. Rao?" I pressed the dress against my body and brushed it.

It was the most beautiful dress I'd ever seen. I

didn't understand the numerical sizing and tried to stretch it over my small frame.

"Mrs. Rao?" I had heard the name called out the first time, but didn't realize it was targeted to me until the light tap on my shoulder had me spinning around.

It was the waiter from the restaurant Raj and I had gone to.

He smiled at me, but not in the way Raj did—not in the way that clearly showed an ulterior motive. His dimples deepened, and he ran his hand through his thick, shiny, light brown hair.

"That's a really nice dress. I'm betting that's your color." I stood there silently, unable to speak or even think of a response.

"I'm Kai, from the restaurant…" He pointed to himself, thinking I didn't recognize the kindest person I'd encountered in my time here.

Swallowing, I reached my hand out. "Hello. I remember. You can just call me Gia." He looked down at my hand and grinned, taking it and shaking it lightly.

"Gia."

His hand was warm, unlike Raj's. His touch felt safe—also unlike Raj's. Releasing it, I placed the dress back on the rack.

"Not getting it?" Kai asked curiously.

"I don't know where I'd wear it. It's so… fancy." I

spoke slowly, trying to annunciate each word clearly to cover up the accent laced in my words.

"I'm sure Dr. Rao would take you somewhere nice, and there's always the restaurant." He smiled with mischief.

Laughing, I lifted it back into my arms. "I don't understand this sizing." I shrugged.

"Hmm… let me see." Kai rubbed his chin dramatically and looked me over from head to toe, which made my heart race.

"I bet you're a size two." He helped me look through the rows and grabbed one. Handing it over, he nodded proudly. "Definitely a two."

Pinching my lips to the side, I looked at his pretty blue eyes. "You must have a lot of experience in women and their sizing." I felt embarrassed as soon as I said it and couldn't believe how I was behaving. Taking a step back, my shoulders tightened.

"I do," he said without a hitch.

I was sick of men and their bullshit.

"I'm going to go check out now, but good to see you." I smiled with all my teeth.

He reached his hand out and grabbed my arm. "No, no… Gia. I have experience because I'm the oldest brother of three little sisters." He let out a laugh.

Blowing out a breath of air, I felt terrible. I was letting my own toxic marriage and perspective of controlling, misogynistic men cloud my opinion of every man.

"Hey, are you hungry? I'd love to make you some fettuccini alfredo." He walked with me to the cash register.

My stomach was growling, and I figured I'd probably never get this opportunity again.

Raj told me he'd pick me up in three hours from Paige's Coffee Shop. I had time to eat and grab some more items.

"I would love to, but I..." I started as the cashier handed me my bag.

"I won't tell him." Kai's eyes narrowed as he looked around us. "I give you my word."

In that moment, I knew Kai had to know things about my husband. Remembering that he didn't recognize who I was, because he was expecting my sister, had me realize he also had to know Amara.

I had to get him to tell me everything. I was now looking into the eyes of the only person in this world who could help me. The only person in this world that knew him and them.

We walked side by side down the road without speaking. I kept a decent distance while looking around to make sure I didn't see his hearse.

Once we got to the restaurant, Kai unlocked the door. I didn't know waiters had the key to restaurants.

It was empty, with no other workers or customers. "We don't open until noon." He looked over his shoulder and waved me inside.

"Oh, it's fine... There isn't a chef, and the owner may get upset if we are here." I grew nervous as he shut the door behind us.

"If you're uncomfortable, I can leave the door open?" Kai offered politely. Hesitating, I knew I couldn't risk Raj seeing us here together. I lived in a house that was cursed, so being in a restaurant with a stranger was the least of my concerns.

"No. It's okay." I followed behind him and we went to the kitchen.

"Here, take a seat." Kai pulled a chair away from the stoves before getting fresh ingredients and some pots out.

"Wait... are you the chef?"

Smiling as he began to work, he nodded. "The owner, the chef, and sometimes the waiter. Your... husband doesn't know that because he has only seen me wait tables when we are understaffed. He doesn't seem like the kind of man who'd care to get to know someone." Kai looked at me.

"Kai, this is amazing. I'm... I'm shocked."

"My mother loved cooking. She taught me everything I knew. Then when she passed, I was even more grateful because I was eighteen with three little sisters looking to me for food." He rolled his sleeves up, showing the intricate tattoos on his forearms.

"I… I'm so sorry about your loss." I hated how I kept stammering, but I had never been alone with a man who wasn't either my father or my husband, yet in this moment, I had also never felt so comfortable. So, at ease. Not every man was a wolf waiting to hunt its prey.

"Would you like me to help?" I offered. I only knew how to cook Indian food and basic things, like boiling eggs.

"No, no. You just relax." He was moving around the kitchen quickly, and the aroma that filled the air had my stomach growling even more.

"What about your father?" I asked nervously.

"He left us and never looked back." Shrugging, he continued to cook, and our conversation shifted to how Raj and I met.

I explained the concept of how an arranged marriage was completely normal in India, and even amongst many cultures around the world. It was actually strange or taboo to fall in love without your parents arranging who you would love.

Kai finished cooking and brought two hefty servings of fettuccini alfredo and garlic bread to the table. My mouth was watering as he adjusted a small fresh flower in a vase between us. I didn't want to think too far into it. He was simply being friendly; he knew I was a married woman.

"I can't believe you are here. You…"

"We don't look alike, I know." I swirled the noodles around my fork and grabbed the napkin after a splatter of sauce went around my lips. "I can't believe you got to know her." I looked up sadly at Kai.

He placed his fork down and leaned back in his chair. "They used to come in here all the time, and then suddenly, they stopped. Raj would come in and get takeout, but he would be short-tempered or avoid eye contact. It was really strange."

"Did you ever see her when she was, um… pregnant?" I stopped eating.

Kai's eyes shot up to mine. "Amara was pregnant?"

My stomach tumbled. Was I wrong? The ultrasound photo had her name, date of birth, and a clear image of a baby.

"I believe she was. I don't know anything about my sister's life here because… well, she never called and her letters were all so formal and screened by Raj. For all I know, he could have written them. Kai, I know this is a lot because I don't know you, and you don't know me, but you're the only person who knows all of us. I think I am in danger with Raj. That house…"

• • •

Kai put his hand up, stopping me from continuing. "I'll do anything you need me to, Gia. I wish I had called the police when I noticed she never came into town. I should have asked Raj but… I didn't. I didn't think it was my place to, but I felt something was off and you know that house it just…" He took a sip of water before looking back at me.

"You know about the Rao Estate?" I whispered, feeling my heart crash against my chest.

Kai laced his fingers together. "Everyone knows that place is haunted. The cemetery, Raj burying the nameless there, and what happened with his father… It's just a recipe for horror. I don't know how Amara lived there, and I don't know how you do, either. You need to get out, Gia."

"Raj's father? Wasn't he and his wife involved in a car accident? Raj's mother is still with us, barely, but still there."

Kai ran his hand through his hair and now, I knew it was an anxious tendency. "That's the story. But the strange thing is, the day of their car accident, Raj was the one who received the bodies. He was the one who incinerated his father, and no one ever saw his mother after that. He said she was alive, and that he'd be caring for her in their home, which had hospital-grade care. No one thought twice. They assumed the quiet, smart doctor who gave the deceased without family or friends a final resting place was an innocent, good man… but there's nothing in this world that has me convinced that house and that man are up to something. I don't think his mother is really alive. I think he staged the whole accident." Kai pushed the breadbasket to me.

My throat went dry as I thought about Mami.

"No, I take…care of her. I take care of his mother." I whispered so lowly that I knew I was convincing myself more than him.

Kai looked at me with pity in his eyes.

"I think he killed my sister, and I think she was pregnant. There's this clanking in the house that echoes all night. I finally found a room downstairs where it's louder, but there's shelves lining the walls and I can't move it all on my own." I took a piece of bread and ripped some off before eating it.

"Kai, I think my sister's soul is haunting the Rao Estate because I think Raj did something to her and her baby. Their baby." Knowing I needed someone who was sound of mind to discuss this with me, I asked, "Do you believe in spirits and ghosts?"

Kai's eyes looked wet as he rested his chin in his hand. "I do. I don't think there's an explanation for everything in the world. I don't think that when we die, all souls find a safe haven. Most people don't believe in ghosts because they don't want to admit that there's something bigger, scarier, and inexplicable out there, completely out of our control."

"If you need a place to hide out, Gia. I have a place. I…"

Wiping my mouth, I thought about how much of an escape this could be for me. But there was a tugging that made me need to go back to the Rao Estate. If I left Raj, if I disappeared, he'd hunt me down. He'd make sure my parents were ruined, and I didn't know what kind of life that would be either way.

"I appreciate that, Kai. I really do. But I have to find out what happened to my sister, her baby, and save Raj's mom. This is all really complicated. My parents have a farm in India and Raj supports it, meaning he supports them. So many things are woven together which makes cutting the thread all that harder. I don't know if I'm ready to undo everything." A tear rolled down my cheek as I stood.

Kai's face dropped as he ran his hands through his hair. Lost in his own thoughts, I wondered what else he knew that he was hesitant to tell me.

"Can I help you clean this up?" I tugged out the credit card but froze. "I'll wash the dishes and help you prepare to open if you don't mind…"

"I would never accept money from you, Gia. I

know he'd see the charge." Kai stood and nodded for me to follow him to the back.

Unlocking a safe, he took out an envelope and handed it to me. "Hide it in your bag with your dress. I'd recommend buying more clothes so he isn't suspicious of your shopping trip. If you need a place to hide or stay, I'm here, Gia."

Loosening my shoulder, I licked my lips. "Why do you want to help me?"

Sticking the envelope inside my bag, Kai leaned in closer. "I could have helped her. I could have saved her."

Kai patted my arm. "I'm never going to be the person who just watches someone fight for their life. I want to be the person who helps them live their life."

I LEFT Kai's restaurant and made my way down the street. I didn't have much time left. I quickly went into another boutique and picked out basics, along with a warm coat. Once I was done, I asked the cashier where the coffee shop was and made my way to it. I knew I couldn't be late for Raj to pick me up. I walked in and stumbled back. He was already there, sitting in the corner with a drink, staring straight at me.

"Hello, wife," he said as soon as I reached his table. "I see you've learned how to be a doctor's wife very quickly." He let out a dry laugh, eyeing my bags.

"If it's all too much, I can take them back. I'm sorry." I felt frazzled, but his face softened.

He pointed to the seat across from him. "Gia, it

makes me happy that I could provide for you. I hope you picked out some nice things. I just booked our tickets to New York." He turned his phone and showed me the confirmation.

"Thank you, and I did. It was nice to get some clothing that wasn't... hers." I scratched at my neck and watched for Raj's reaction.

He took another sip of his coffee and slowly shook his head. "I know it has been unfair and cruel for you to live the way you have, Gia. I am hoping that with this honeymoon, we can also have a fresh start."

Rubbing my arms, I brushed my finger across my bottom lip. There has always been three people in our marriage—my husband, my sister, and then me. It was the normal to me. I knew from the moment my father sat me down that I'd never be in a real marriage... I just didn't know how depraved it could be.

"I'm excited for our fresh start." I blew out a breath of air. Before I knew it, we were back in the hearse with the morbid odor filling my nostrils.

My eyes stung as I pressed my thumb into my palm to prevent myself from vomiting.

Raj was completely unbothered. I glanced over my shoulder but there was nothing alarming. It was simply the fact that he'd carried so many dead bodies in this car that the scent was embedded into it.

I could see the estate from a distance below at the

end of the winding driveway. I didn't want to go back; I wanted to stay in town. I wanted to stay with Kai and run or hide. I wanted to start a new life for myself. And I would. I just had to tie up some loose ends and save Mami, too.

When we got home, Raj said he had things to take care of and that I should check on Mami and start packing for New York. I knew he wanted to distract me from whatever he was doing, but still, I obliged. I couldn't risk him becoming frustrated with me.

Carrying my bags upstairs, I looked down at the banister. Stopping midway, I squinted and leaned closer to the worn wood. Tracing the deep lines, I realized they were markings from age. Digging my nails into them, I outlined each one and could tell they were nail imprints. Gasping, I took a step back and glanced down. Someone was either dragged downstairs or upstairs against their will.

Was that someone still here?

———

I opened her door carefully and placed my bags down. Her eyes were wide open in the darkness, the whites of them almost reflective. Turning the small oil-burning lantern on, I looked at her. "Mami, are you hungry?"

Her thin lips were cracked, and she continued to stare straight ahead.

She already looked like a corpse. "Mami, I need you to help me understand so many things. But did you tell Raj that you want him to help you… die?" I sank onto her bed and placed her wrinkled, dry hand in mine.

Slowly turning her head, she opened her lips and said with a small smile curving on her lips, "You can't kill a dead person."

My body went cold as she dug her fingers deeper into my hand.

"Mami… you aren't dead," I whimpered.

She laughed loudly as drool trickled down her lips. Falling back, I pried her hand off mine and grabbed my bags before sprinting out.

I didn't think I could save someone who already thought they were dead. But Mami needed help. She needed a doctor, a nursing home, proper care. After the accident, she came here rather than to a proper medical facility.

I went to my old bedroom and slowly began unpacking my new clothes. Shutting the door and locking it as silently as possible, I tugged out the envelope full of cash that Kai had given me.

Lifting the mattress, I hid it underneath, thankful for the kindness of a man who I had no ties to and could never repay.

As I sat on the floor thinking about everything, I heard something. A clanking, a faint voice. Crawling on all fours to the vent that was by my old bed, I pressed my ear against it. I couldn't make out what it was since it sounded so distant.

But it sounded like a voice. A woman's voice.

"Hello?" I whispered through the vent.

The clanking stopped. The voice stopped.

Was my sister in this house? Was she alive? Pushing myself off the ground, I gripped the banister and ran down the stairs, my footsteps thumping against each one. I didn't even care at all that Mami and Raj could hear the urgency of my movements.

Sprinting down the hallway, I saw the door open. Slowing down, I walked in and saw that the shelves had been moved.

There was another door, so small I had to crouch down to go through it. As soon as I stood, my jaw dropped.

It looked nothing like the rest of the house, and was frigid. The bright fluorescent lights were blinding, and a steel operation table laid in the middle.

What was this? There were oversized black and white portraits of a few men in white coats. Squinting I brushed my fingers against the plaques underneath each image.

Dr. Noah Wimberly and Dr. Ian Ivory. Who were

these men? Why was my husband idolizing them? My stomach tumbled as I took a deep breath in, regretfully.

The scent was a mix of decomposing bodies and…

Cold fingers brushed against my back and my spine immediately straightened as the lump in my throat felt like it was blocking my airways.

"Hello, darling." His voice felt like needles pricking into my skin as he physically turned me around while my body tensed further.

He was dressed in scrubs with latex gloves covering his hands.

"Raj, I…"

Pressing his covered index finger over my lips, he hushed me.

"It's okay. Curiosity is a sign of brilliance. And you, my Gia, aren't stupid like your older sister is."

Is.

Present tense. He used present tense to talk about Amara. She was here. She wasn't some spirit haunting us. She was alive, and I knew it. I knew the pull and tug of this house was her pleading with me to save her.

"Raj, what is this?" I was trembling, praying I wouldn't collapse from the extreme terror coursing through my veins.

Looking at all the shiny, stainless-steel surgical instruments, I didn't know if my curiosity had just sent me to an early grave.

"It's where I prepare the bodies to bury in the cemetery or burn. You know what your problem is, Gia?" Raj walked closer to me as I stumbled backward into a corner.

Clenching my teeth, I felt like prey officially being trapped by its predator.

"You think I'm the enemy. From day one, you have always thought I was the enemy, and here we are… Have I ever hurt you? Have I chained you up and starved you? Have I thrown you out on the streets?"

I hated how he was right. He hadn't done any of those things to that degree. "No."

"You always assume I'm this monster trying to hurt you because you've completely convinced yourself that I hurt your sister. But the truth is, I will never love someone the way I loved Amara. We were trying so hard to be happy. We almost were, you know? But then, she failed me. She ruined everything. She…" Raj abruptly stopped and filled the space between us. "She could have ended this all." He dropped his head down.

I looked around the room. Part of me felt relief, and a second part felt disappointment. I thought my sister would be here, like some kind of horror movie situation where she'd be held hostage, waiting for me to save her. But it wasn't true. I was holding on to false hope. She was dead, but maybe that was better than living in this hell.

"Why don't you lay on the table, my beloved?" Raj began walking closer. I swallowed the lump in my throat and shook my head.

"No, Raj." My bottom lip quivered as he cornered me and the cool steel jammed into my backside.

"Sit, I just made a new batch of something for you to try." His thick brows lowered as he reached for the travel thermos sitting on the counter. Twisting the lid opened, he used the top to fill up with something steaming hot.

"Drink this. It will calm you." He watched me intently as I pressed my lips together tightly.

"What is it?" I questioned looking at the dark liquid.

"Life. If you don't drink it there will be repercussions."

Reaching out with my hand trembling I took the cup and closed my eyes.

"Drink!" He yelled out.

I jerked back and immediately pressed the cup against my lips. It was bitter and clumpy.

Gagging as tears rolled down my face, he continued to yell until I drank it all.

Laughter echoed as I slid off the table and ran out of the room until I made it to the restroom.

Vomit poured out of my mouth and something was wrapped around my tongue.

A piece of long black hair tinged with henna that only Amara used to dye her hair with.

Dropping to the floor, I hugged my knees into my chest.

I think my husband just made me drink a cup of my sister's remains.

THE DAYS FLEW by in a blur, and Raj had postponed our New York trip for another week. He didn't take me anywhere, and truthfully, I stayed by Mami's side. I knew he was up to something. He kept referring to her as a burden. He said it was her wish all along to die a peaceful death and not live this tragic life. I no longer felt like I was alive at all, but rather simply just a corpse walking around. Raj kept mumbling to himself about saving Mami's soul and helping her find peace.

I didn't believe him. I would never believe him. "Mami, would you want to maybe leave this house with me for a little bit?" I whispered to her, clutching her aged hands in mine.

I had given her a bath, brushed her hair, begged her

to eat, and had spent some time reading a book to her today.

She looked at me with a dribble of spit dripping down her chin. Her eyes lowered as they filled with tears. In Hindi, she said, "I will never leave her. I will never leave her!" Each word grew louder and louder.

Her grip around my hands tightened. "Who, Mami? Who do you not want to leave behind?"

She tilted her head slightly and groaned, "You should have never come here. She could have saved us all." She began to sob uncontrollably.

Amara. She didn't want to leave my sister. My dead sister.

Nothing unusual had happened in the past few days, and coincidentally, I was sleeping better. Part of me was beginning to think my own mind was, in fact, my worst enemy.

Standing, I left Mami's room. There was nothing I could do to help her. She was convinced my sister's spirit was roaming this house. She loved her the way Raj did, but that was Amara. She had a way of gliding into a room and everyone being smitten by her. Not me… I had a way of gliding into rooms and leaving chaos behind.

Going to the balcony, I gripped the broken stone

railing and looked out to the ocean. There was nothing here for me to do. My sister's soul would never be at rest or peace. She was bound in these walls, and I'd never know what really happened to her. As thoughts circled through my mind, I shuddered. A strange taste in my mouth grew and suddenly, I gripped my stomach as nausea twirled inside me. I had decided to not think of the warm drink Raj forced me to drink but since then the nausea and vomiting hadn't let up.

My upper body began to jerk as I gagged. Leaning over the railing, I vomited profusely and my eyes stung.

I hadn't eaten anything unusual. I was sleeping deeper and more. My head felt light as I pulled up and wiped my lips. Opening my eyes wider, everything was growing hazy.

"Oh no," I breathed out as realization flooded through me. My feet ached as I sprinted across the rough floors and into our bathroom. Tugging the medicine cabinet open, I saw the boxes of ovulation and pregnancy tests. It had been the greatest gift that Raj had stopped forcing me to take them. But now, here I was, willingly crouching over one, knowing my world and everything I was planning would burn to ashes.

Forcing myself to take deep breaths, I clenched my eyes shut as I counted five seconds before pulling the stick out from under me.

Carrying it to the counter, I placed it down and washed my hands. I didn't move and counted one hundred and eighty seconds out until I looked down and slapped my hand over my mouth.

"No, no… no." I shook as I lifted it and saw the two darkened lines.

I was pregnant with a monster's child.

The child he wanted more than anything. But what terrified me the most was my sister probably stood in this very same spot, holding this test, and nine months later, something happened to both her and her child that landed her in an urn. What if all this time, her ashes were mixed with her child's? Were my parents holding both their daughter and grandchild in that urn?

I couldn't have this baby. No, I couldn't be bound to Raj. I couldn't let him hurt a child that didn't ask to be born into this demented house.

Brushing my hand across my stomach, I rolled my lips together.

I was pregnant. In some sick way, a strange feeling of happiness, for the very first time, wrapped around me.

I think it was because, for the first time in a very long time, I wasn't alone.

———————

I laid in the library for the rest of the day and stared at the countless books surrounding me. Wuthering Heights laid on my belly, and I took a deep breath in before releasing it slowly. Nausea kept creeping inside me, and I kept fixating on the metallic taste on my tongue.

How was I going to hide this from Raj? I brushed my hand across my abdomen, which was curved more inward than outward. I had lost a significant amount of weight ever since moving here due to the limited food, not to mention the endless anxiety and stress… I closed my eyes. I wanted more of Kai's fettuccini alfredo.

A small smile curved across my lips, but tipped downward almost instantly. I didn't know if I was overanalyzing his kindness into flirtation. I just knew with certainty that there was no way a man with so much ambition, charisma, and life ahead of him would have any interest in helping a married, pregnant woman. I thought about the money upstairs and how I had hidden it.

But it wasn't enough. It wasn't enough for me to run away from this haunted fortress and know I could be safe or healthy while pregnant. The sliver of joy I felt from knowing a small, beautiful life was growing inside me went away just as fast because ultimately, this baby was now a ball and chain.

My thoughts quickly faded as the door creaked

open. Quickly sitting up, I heard his heavy footsteps enter the house.

"Hi." He waved at me. He was wearing scrubs and, looking at them carefully, I could see stains splattered across them.

Deep red stains.

"Hello," I said awkwardly.

"I need to tell you something." His voice shifted and he moved closer to me.

I grabbed an old throw pillow from the couch and clutched it in front of my body protectively.

Sinking next to me, I could smell the same stench that was embedded in the hearse he drove.

Death, formaldehyde, and blood.

"Gia, your father..." he started. My mind went numb just as those three words left his lips.

"No, no..." I chanted. The one person in the world I'd have wanted to tell about this baby... the one person in this world who ever loved me.

"He's not dead." Raj opened his palm, and I looked down at it.

Pursing my quivering lips, I pressed my hand into his. "He's been diagnosed with a rare heart condition. The treatment is costly, but without it he will die within the year." For the first time, I could see Raj in the light of a physician. The way he was delivering such alarming and life-altering news in such a calm way made me realize that perhaps it wasn't the "doctor" in him, but rather the sociopath in him.

Tears streamed down my cheeks as I absorbed everything Raj continued to discuss. He went into detail about the heart condition and how he had spoken with my mother, father, and even the physician in India treating him.

"I'll book tickets for us to visit them, but we can't go until... Well, until things with my mother are settled."

"Settled?" My hands shook.

"You remember I told you about her wishes. Well, this isn't a state where physician-assisted euthanasia is legal. I have..."

"You're going to kill your mother?" I cried out. I knew what he meant all those times but, in this moment, I needed to hear him say it. I needed him to say the words as I wept over my own parent fighting for his life.

But he didn't say anything; instead, he wiped the tears off my face and kissed me.

I hated the way I wasn't strong enough to push him off of me, save his mother and run away.

"She wants peace, Gia. We can't watch her suffer any longer. We can't. This house has ripped her down. There's been so much pain in these walls that have closed in on her. She brings reminders of pain... ones you know nothing about, Gia." Raj pressed his forehead against mine.

"My father might die before we go back to India," I whimpered selfishly.

Raj shook his head before pulling away slightly. "I'm paying the best doctor in the city to care for him. I've already sent the money, and everything is in line for your father to be cared for. With treatment, he has years to come."

My lips parted in shock as I stared into Raj's deep brown eyes. Tears rapidly filled my eyes as I tilted my head.

He cared?

CHAPTER
TWENTY-SEVEN

I WOKE up earlier than Raj and raced down the hall to the bathroom closest to Mami's room. Clutching the yellowed toilet, I vomited so hard I swore my ribs were breaking. Every smell in the house was even more intense, and every step I took felt like the world was shaking. I trembled as I flushed the toilet, knowing nothing was left in my stomach beyond acid, which would burn on its way out.

I laid my head on the toilet seat, not caring how it probably hadn't been cleaned well in years. My body was exhausted. It was hard to sleep at night, and then the vomiting was getting worse.

The bell jingled.

Groaning, I pushed myself up and washed my hands before gargling some water.

Wiping the sweat beads off my forehead, I opened

Mami's door and gagged. The scent of feces was suffocating. Scrunching my nose, I pulled open the curtains, which immediately released a cloud of dust. Coughing, all I wanted to do was lay down in a tub of warm water and scrub myself after brushing my teeth.

Mami whispered something and a sliver of sun grazed her face.

"Mami, I'll give you a bath. You should have rung your bell if you needed help to use the bathroom." I immediately felt guilty about the annoyance lacing my words and the impatience that was palpable.

But I wasn't qualified to do this. Taking care of a woman I hardly knew, who was in serious need of proper medical care around the clock, was something I shouldn't have been forced to carry. Mami slowly turned toward me.

Reaching her hand out, she placed her palm against my abdomen. I looked down in disbelief. I had the bathroom door shut and the water running when I was throwing up.

"How… how did you…"

"She told me," Mami said softly in Hindi.

I shook my head and moved away. She had to have heard me in the bathroom. I wouldn't believe any of this.

Pointing to a basket in the corner of the room, Mami asked me to bring it over to her.

Lifting it up, I dug into it, seeing random crochet items. "First, let me clean you. Then you can have this."

Mami's cataract-clouded eyes filled with embarrassment. "It's okay. I'm sorry I'm not good at…"

Something shifted in that moment—Mami looked at me differently. I gave her a sponge bath, I brushed her hair, and I even painted her nails with an old bottle hidden away in Amara's things. It was mostly dried out, but I had mixed a little remover with it, and it was good enough. Her thin lips broke into a smile as she looked at her hands. It was worth the agonizing pain I felt smelling nail polish and feces while newly pregnant. Once dried, she pointed to her basket again.

Adding a few pillows behind her body, I nestled the basket next to her and handed her the needlepoint items.

"Don't tell him." Her voice cracked as she began working on something.

I sat at the foot of her bed. "Why not?" I asked quietly, knowing her reasoning would probably wreck me.

Her fingers were moving abnormally fast, but she wasn't looking down as she stitched. She was looking directly at me, as if she wasn't the one moving the needles…

Her eyes widened before she shot straight up and

smiled slowly at me. "If it's a girl, she'll be dead. If it's a boy, he'll be offered." Mami's voice sounded different, yet familiar.

"Run, run, little butterfly."

Jumping up, my body shook as I looked down at her fingers moving. Grabbing the needlepoint from her hands, I cried out.

"Amara!" It was an almost-complete butterfly with one broken wing.

Shaking the needlepoint violently, I screamed, "What is this? Why are you doing this to me?" I couldn't believe this was happening to me.

Tears blurred my vision, but it wasn't tears of sadness, rather anger. My nose was running as Mami stared at me with a smile.

"Save them..." she said, and just like that, Mami collapsed backward with her eyes rolling into her head.

My entire body trembled as I felt stuck in the same place. "Mami?" I murmured. Taking a step closer, I puffed my cheeks and put one foot in front of the other before leaning down. Reaching out, I placed my hand on her chest, but couldn't feel anything. "Oh no... no..." I blew out air and began to cry.

She was dead.

Sinking down to the floor, I sobbed at the loss of the only other person in this house who provided me some form of belief that survival was possible here. I sobbed at the loss of the only person in this house who could have provided me some form of insight on the hell that was rampaging through the walls of this so-called home.

But just as I choked on my tears, a sudden movement startled me as Mami slapped her hand across mine and dug her nails into my flesh.

Letting out a scream, I looked up at her, but she was still lying flat. A terrifying, large smile plastered across of her face.

"Mami." I stood hopefully while shaking from fear. Bending over, my hand was still tightly gripped in hers. "Mami," I said louder, and as soon as I did, her eyes shot opened and she screamed. She screamed so loudly that the air from my lungs was knocked out as I stumbled back, yet dangled from her hand not releasing mine.

I called out for help, which was simply foolish considering there wasn't anyone here to save me.

But heavy footsteps echoed behind as I tried with all my might to rip Mami's hand from mine.

"Gia? Gia…" Raj appeared and attempted to release Mami's hand from me, though he was unsuccessful. Foam built at her lips as she spoke in a deep, hoarse voice completely different from her own. "Run, run, little butterfly. Run, run."

Raj glanced at me with sweat lining his forehead. "Close your eyes, Gia. Close them!"

My heart was pounding as I slammed them shut and heard something indescribable.

Something had splattered against my face and chest. Raj was breathing vociferously as I gradually opened my eyes.

The screams that left my body were unrecognizable. Mami's hand that was once gripping my wrist was now laying on the bed, completely detached from her body. There was blood everywhere as Raj's arm lifted into the air and, with one rapid motion, dug a dirtied blade into her body repeatedly, with nothing more than a smile and dashes of blood painted across his face.

I didn't feel present in the moment. It was as if I were watching myself in a scene that was a dream… a nightmare. The blend of their screams deafened me until Raj looked over at me and licked his bottom lip, which was covered in his mother's blood.

I ran.

I ran faster than I thought my body could. Everything grew fuzzy around me as my body broke into a cold sweat, and I slid across the flooring to my old bedroom. Grabbing the envelope of cash, I sprinted out and was racing down the curved stairs two at a time.

"Gia! Gia!"

I looked over my shoulder and saw my husband covered in his mother's blood.

"My love, stop right now!" He was chasing after me. Adrenaline coursed through my body as I tugged the door open and kept moving. My feet ached against the winding driveway crafted of only gravel, as the thin white gown decorated with small, pale pink flowers floated around me. "Sweetheart!" His voice grew hoarse as he belted out my name.

Looking back once more, I saw he had stopped running. His hands were on his hips, and he was walking to the hearse.

I was already exhausted, and I knew he was going to hunt me down. Pushing myself, I kept going, even as I heard the car crunch against the gravel behind me, filling the space between us far too quickly.

I knew that once I veered off the road that I was almost at risk of getting lost and reaching nowhere. We were caged in by the ocean on one side and dense woods on the other.

Raj began honking at me wildly, shouting out of his window. My body was aching as I cut right and ran into the woods. He slammed his brakes and the hearse screeched against the road.

My feet were cut, bleeding, and in agonizing pain as the fallen branches, leaves, and rocks crushed under my feet that were already raw from the gravel.

I could hear Raj behind me, sprinting, but then, by the grace of whatever superpower there had to be somewhere in this universe, I heard him yell out in pain as he tripped and fell.

I grew more winded and my abdomen cramped, and just as I was about to slow down, a small, yellow butterfly floated across me and fluttered forward.

Run, run, my little butterfly.

Even though I was sweating, chills decorated my arms as I chased it, hearing Amara's haunting voice ricochet through the dense trees.

I couldn't hear Raj's aggressive words or see how everything looked the same around me. I knew I was running parallel to the road, which led to the city. That would have to be enough. Anywhere but with him had to be enough.

CHAPTER
TWENTY-EIGHT

I STOOD on the bustling sidewalk, covered in splatters of blood, dirt, and tears staring blankly at the bystanders, who were looking at me in disbelief but not stopping.

No one asked if I needed help. No one asked if I was alright. No, I was a mere spectacle. Instead, they were drawing their phones out to snap a photo of me as if I were some animal on display at the zoo, then immediately picked up their pace to race by.

Clearing my throat, which felt like sandpaper, I walked up to an elderly woman. Her eyes widened and shot to the side as she saw me approach her.

"Hi, could you please tell me were Kai's restaurant is? It's an Italian restaurant." My voice quivered as the wrinkles in her face deepened.

"Do you need help, child?"

The simple statement had me break into a sob. "Please don't call the police." I looked at my gown and knew I still had Mami's blood on my face, too.

I also knew the police would never believe me if they saw me in this state. By the time they went back to the estate, Raj would have cleaned everything up. He knew I was on the run, looking for help. He probably assumed it was the police I was searching for.

The old woman tilted her head slightly and nodded. "I hope he got what he deserved." She assumed I had hurt my husband or that he had hurt me.

"Not yet," I whimpered.

Gripping into her cane, her thin lips curved upward. "Kai's restaurant is called Farfalla. He recently renamed it. It's right down this street." She pointed.

"Farfalla." I nodded. "Thank you." Turning away, I wrapped my arms around myself before hurrying through the crowds and avoiding the gasps. I felt invisible my entire life but now, I was wishing for it more than ever.

––––––––

"Gia." The way he said my name seared into my heart and broke me. He threw down the towel from his shoulder on the counter and raced to me. Dropping my head down from embarrassment, I saw his forearms covered in tattoos as his hands gripped mine.

"What… what happened?" He guided me to a chair before quickly leaving to lock the front door and turn the open sign back over.

"I didn't know who else to go to. I have no one," I cried as the tears fell into my lap.

Dropping to his knees in front of me, he looked up. His pale blue eyes were full of concern and confusion. "He's a monster. You're safe. I'll protect you, I promise." Cupping my face, he sighed.

"You knew her. You knew my sister." I sniffled and wiped under my eyes.

Kai licked his bottom lip and stood. "Come with me. Let's get you changed and fed. Then I'll tell you whatever I can remember."

My legs were shaking from hunger and exhaustion. Kai came back with a pair of socks and leaned down to lift my legs, covering each foot with a sock.

"Let's go home." He helped me stand, and I leaned into him as he put his arm around me.

I didn't think I'd ever have a home. I didn't think I'd ever know what one was after leaving India, but in this moment, all I knew was that this would be the closest thing to ever experiencing one. A stranger's home felt safer than any place I'd ever lived. My heart ached for myself.

We got into Kai's car and drove five minutes down the road to a tall, shiny building. He pulled into a parking garage that required him to punch in numbers to open the gate. Looking back, I watched the heavy steel slam back down into the concrete. A small taste of relief spread through me.

I'm safe.

I appreciated the silence between us as we went into the elevator, and Kai pressed a button labeled PH.

I'd never been to an apartment or condo building before. Most of them were in the big cities, and something our village didn't have.

The doors opened right into a living space. It was absolutely gorgeous. My lips parted in shock as I looked inside the modern, well-lit home. "Kai, this is yours?" It was such a stupid question, but he was a humble man who I only just learned was the owner of the restaurant.

"It is." He waved me in and went to the kitchen. Filling up a glass of water, he slid it over to me. "Can I ask you who's blood that is?" His voice dropped and the pause in between each word had my heart slowing.

"Raj killed his mother. She… she's gone." Closing

my eyes, I clenched them even tighter as I watched the knife cut into the same body that had given him life.

Kai looked shocked, but not in the way I expected.

"Raj's mother?" he repeated as he froze in place with a pan in his hand.

Nodding, I swallowed the entire glass of water, feeling the coolness glaze my throat.

"Raj's mother died in the same car accident his father did." He said.

My breathing hitched as I leaned back in the chair. Letting out a dry laugh, I shook my head. "I cared for her from the moment I walked through those doors. I bathed, fed, and talked to her. She was paralyzed from the waist down. But she was living and breathing until Raj, my husband, murdered her in front of my eyes. Her voice had changed... it sounded like Amara's." I choked in disbelief that these words were toppling out from my lips with ease.

"Wait here for a minute." Kai left the kitchen. I stood and made my way to the sink, then turned it on and quickly washed my hands. Scrubbing between my fingers and underneath my fingernails, I watched the dirt and blood swirl into the oversized, stark white sink.

Kai came back out carrying a yellow folder. Tossing it onto the kitchen island, he looked at me. "First, if you'd like, you can shower and change. I've set everything out in the bathroom while I cook for you, and then we can sort everything else out."

"What is that?" I took a paper towel and dried my hands.

"Shower, eat, and then we can get to it. Please?" I felt nervous as I stood in the home of a man I didn't know. I couldn't help but think of the irony. I knew Kai more than I knew the man I married. I wished so badly that I could have been a girl who got to go to college, educate herself, get a job, and be able to support herself. Instead, I was set up for dependence and failure. I was set up to be someone's doormat and victim.

"Okay."

Kai led me to the luxurious bathroom that was attached to what looked like a guest room. Two of the four walls offered seamless views of the city I had never known or explored.

"Do you need…" He paused. "Any help?" We both winced at the question, but I knew he was trying to be kind.

"I'm fine. I'll figure it out." Shutting the door behind him, he left, and I stared at the girl in the reflection. I didn't recognize her gaunt face, her sunken eyes, or the lackluster waves of raven hair. Instead, I recognized the blood splattered across her cheeks and right by her bottom lip. I recognized the sadness lurking in her brown eyes and the loss of hope depleted from them.

Shuddering, I went to the shower and turned it on. It was like rain falling from the sky. I assumed this is what the American dream truly was. And it was beautiful. Peeling the disgusting nightgown off my body, I walked into the shower and for the first time, I felt my body getting clean. Not just from the dirt, blood, and sweat, but from the pain and horror I had been through.

Brushing my hand across my abdomen, I had forgotten there was another life inside me. I couldn't even protect myself. What could I even offer this child? A murderer as a father, a completely dependent, clueless mother in a country that wasn't even her own? I belonged nowhere.

Sinking to the floor, I put my head in between my knees and took a deep breath. As soon as I closed my eyes, my body tightened.

I could see Mami's body being cut up like a loaf of bread or meat. Death was strange. I hadn't experienced it in my life beyond my grandparents and then my sister. But with Amara, I don't think I'd ever believed she was dead. I didn't see her body; I didn't see her withering away with an illness. I didn't get a call from the police. It was all based around a man my family hardly knew, handing us her ashes. Perhaps that's why

I had become obsessed with what had happened to her. I never got the closure I had to have. Mami was dead; she died in front of me. Her voice… her voice sounded just like the sister I loved more than anyone.

Had I officially gone insane?

Forcing myself up, I pumped shampoo into my hands and cleaned my hair before scrubbing my body.

I knew without a doubt that Raj was cleaning up his mother's remains. He had an entire morgue right down the hall from our kitchen. Then he'd look for me, and I knew he'd hunt me down until he found me.

Maybe he'd give up sooner than later… maybe he'd assume I was dead.

Maybe I'd learn how to be dead.

Wasn't I already?

KAI HAD a plate of fettuccini alfredo, garlic bread, and fresh lemonade waiting for me when I came out. The scent of garlic had nausea crashing over me, but the pangs of hunger overtook any pregnancy symptoms. I was wearing Kai's sweatshirt and sweatpants that were both huge on me.

Yet, it was the first time in a long time that I wasn't wearing Amara's hand-me-downs and I felt like my own person.

I was my own person.

"Thank you, Kai. I'm—"

He put his hand up, his cheeks flushed pink. "Please, Gia, I wish I had never let you go back after that day you were in my restaurant. I know what he is and yet, I didn't stop you from going into his trap."

Sinking down in front of the hot meal, I began

eating the way an emaciated animal does when scraps are left in the trash.

Poverty and starvation weren't new concepts to me. My village was full of children begging with small silver bowls for anything. Everyone fought to survive. And here I was, a doctor's wife in the glamorous country of America, starving beyond hunger.

"No one can save me."

I ate in silence, my brain swirling with my mother-in-law's gruesome murder haunting me with every bite.

Once done, I burped and slapped my mouth as Kai smiled.

"I'm… excuse me." Embarrassment flooded over me.

"Gia, you showed up to my restaurant in the middle of downtown wearing a nightgown covered in blood and sweat. A burp is the least of our concerns." Kai waved me over the sleek white sectional and turned the fireplace on. It was all too beautiful. I had heard of girls marrying wealthy men in America— they'd be arranged with the perfect man after matching biodatas, which were essentially folders full of education, hobbies, interests, wealth, and family history. Marriage was nothing more than a business transaction. My parents looked at a so-called wealthy man from across the ocean and threw their daughter at him.

They didn't learn their lesson when that daughter came home in an urn; instead, they gave him another.

Tears filled my eyes as I thought about my parents. My father's medical treatment was being funded by Raj.

How could I be so selfish to let my father die?

"Gia?" Kai's voice sounded distant, which told me he'd been calling my name out multiple times. The ringing in my ear clouded my hearing as I shook my head.

"Sorry," I breathed out and looked at the coffee table that was now neatly covered in rows of paper. Photo images of a woman and man, a car accident, and words I didn't understand.

"What is this?" I padded my fingers against a photo of an older woman.

"That is Padma Rao. Your mother-in-law."

Scoffing, I thought this was some kind of prank. "Kai, I've been caring for my mother-in-law to the point of bathing her. I think I'd know what she looked like."

"Gia, before I opened my restaurant, I was a cop in a nearby town. I moved here six years ago and heard all about the Rao Estate—the hauntings, the cemetery, the peculiar things the tenants did. How isolated it was from the rest of the world, although just outside the city lines." He paused and opened the folder, tugging out documents.

"Curiosity got the best of me, and I had my buddy, Zach, at the station give me these. But after I saw you, I asked him to look into Raj's mother. He looked at me like I was crazy because her body was accounted for."

My heart hammered against my chest precipitously. "If this… this was Raj's mother, then who was the woman I was caring for all this time?"

Kai shrugged. "I don't know. I'm going to give Zach a call later and see if he can go by the estate."

"No!" I panicked. "Did you tell him I was here?"

Kai reached over and brushed my arm. "No, Gia. I didn't say anything about you. But I did ask him to go there and check it out. If what you saw was real, then… there's been a murder and Raj should be locked up. He did something to a woman we don't even know who it is, and he did something to Amara."

I was taken aback. "You knew my sister… you knew her while she was here. What did Raj tell you about her?"

Kai sighed and leaned back against the couch. "They'd come to my restaurant often. No one really knew either of them. To be honest, I don't think Raj had friends in town. The Rao Estate is secluded, and this area is a predominately wealthy, Caucasian area."

"He's a doctor. He's a medical examiner." I brushed my hand across my chin.

"A private one. Apparently, Dr. Raj Rao would get contracted to do work, and he'd specifically never really repeat the hospitals or clinics. He'd drive far out, too. No one knew him, Gia."

"He wanted to stay invisible. Which is already easy to do when no one cares to get to know you, and you don't care to know them."

"This is a pretty conservative city. So yes, it was very advantageous for them to be imperceptible here." Kai licked his lips and looked at me carefully.

"Gia, you should go get some sleep. I'll wake you when Zach calls. Raj can't get to you, I promise. I promise, I'll never let any living person hurt you." Kai stood.

Any living person… What else did Kai know?

———

I slept deeper than I had in months. I woke only twice, when poignant images of Mami's face and Amara's voice trickled in. I touched my face, feeling warmth. Opening my eyes, I saw the sunlight streaming into the room.

Walking to the living room, I saw Kai. Something

smelled divine—the same way the sunshine felt on my face.

"Coffee?" Kai turned with a warm mug. He was wearing gray sweatpants and a fitted white T-shirt.

"I've never had coffee in my life. But yes, please." I sat on the barstool. This was a first, a man serving me. I thought of how appalled all the aunties, uncles, even my own parents would be if they saw this scene.

Kai smiled as he slid the steaming mug of camel-colored coffee to me. I took a long sip before cupping the mug between my palms, warming them. The taste was much different from the mixture of cardamom, ginger and spices that crafted chai.

"Did your friend, the police officer, call?" I asked, unsure if I was prepared for the response.

Kai tossed his head back before blowing out a breath of air. "Raj is looking for you. He was completely frantic about your whereabouts. Gia, they searched the house… and nothing was found. There were no signs of foul play or an elderly woman ever living there."

Rubbing my lips together, I sniffled with anxiety surging through my body. "He's smart. He's done something with her body. He's got a morgue in the house, right by the kitchen! He's burying bodies in the cemetery." Desperation coated each frantic word.

"Zach cross-checked the tombstones, and they

match up with well, lost souls. The unloved, the homeless, the unaccounted. He gave them their final resting place."

Closing my eyes, I knew what I had witnessed. I knew what he had done to Mami. I knew I wasn't crazy.

"So, you think I'm making all of this up?" I cried out.

Kai shook his head and came around the island. "No, Gia. I'm saying he's a mastermind. There's no cause to search into him. But he's searching for you, and from what Zach told me, he's about to blow up the media for you."

I stared at the coffee in front of me. I knew he wouldn't stop until he found me. I knew men like Raj —controlling and possessive in a way that made your stomach curl.

I wasn't his wife; I was his property.

"I can't go back to him, Kai. I know what I saw. I don't know what happened to my sister, but I do know she's haunting the walls of that house. I do know her soul isn't resting." I wiped the tears from my face as Kai watched me plead for my life while sounding mentally unstable.

"You can stay here for as long as you'd like, Gia. I'll never stop protecting you. And most of all, I believe you."

"Kai… I'm pregnant."

His eyes shot to mine. "Does Raj know?"

Shaking my head, I looked away. "No."

Kai pinched his lips to the side. "Then we have to keep it that way."

TWO WEEKS HAD COME and gone. Kai carried guilt on his shoulders that I was "trapped" within the four walls of what I learned was a penthouse. Meanwhile, I had never felt freer in my life. Fresh, hot meals, conversations, and laughter, albeit forced sometimes, because most days I felt like a shallow shell of a human, completely lost and unsure of what my life would become. My stomach was growing, either from the baby or the fact that I was indulging in all the delicacies Kai was bringing home. He bought prenatal vitamins for me, and I even caught him reading a book on pregnancy. I didn't understand the dynamic we shared, but I also didn't have much mental strength to question it. Vomiting and nausea were still a part of my days, and it was too dangerous to go be seen by a doctor, so I learned what I could and repeated what I grew up seeing. Women in the village gave birth all the time without proper medical care, but most of them had mothers, mother-in-laws, husbands, and families to guide them.

After staying with me for a couple of days, I assured Kai I'd be fine, and he would leave early each day. I didn't want him to lose his livelihood over mine. Wrapping myself in the fuzzy robe, I lifted the new cell phone he'd gifted me. I had thought about it endless times but always wondered what I'd say to my parents if I called. I was sure Raj had already called them, and seeing my face plastered on the news a couple of times made it even worse. Raj had done a press conference, standing in front of a camera with his beard trimmed, desolate eyes, and the face of a worried husband.

But no one truly cared.

The perks of that meant no one was looking for me. No one cared to look for a missing brown woman.

Looking out at the city I couldn't explore or learn more about, I sank into the couch and thought about the one number besides Kai's I had memorized.

It was around eleven at night and Kai was working late since the restaurant stayed open until two a.m. on the weekends. I didn't mind, considering Kai let me use his Amazon account to order any books I wanted.

Curling up, I tugged the blanket over me and with shaking fingers, dialed the number.

Something in the pit of my stomach told me to hang up with each ring. But I didn't, and just as I was lifting the phone from my ear, I heard his voice.

Emotion washed over me as soon as he answered.

"Papa," I whimpered.

Silence fell between us. I could picture him standing there in worn house sandals with sweat beads sliding down his temple as he thought about what to say to his only living child.

"Gia, beta." The warmth in his voice wasn't the same; instead, it was replaced with exhaustion.

"Papa, I don't know what Raj told you, but it's bad…. He killed his mother. He killed Amara. I can't go back to him. He will kill me next. That house it's not…" My words were scrambled and scattered as I frantically tried to condense months of hell into a quick sentence, knowing I didn't have much time to convince Papa after I knew with certainty that Raj had probably used his heartbroken hero card on them.

"Gia, stop. Stop, Gia. Are you safe?" he asked, but just as my lips parted to answer, the phone was tugged from him and my mother took over.

"Gia." She was crying. I didn't think I had ever heard my mother cry over me. Not when I fell and got hurt, not when I was deathly ill, not when she waved me off with my dead sister's husband.

For Amara, she always had emotion.

"Tell us where you are, and we will come get you. Papa is booking the tickets now." She was sobbing hysterically. I felt cared about and loved, and when that happens, vulnerability is born.

"I'm pregnant, ma." I knew I had to tell her. It wasn't a secret to be kept.

Silence.

"Tell us where you are…" she asked with concern.

"I'm staying with a friend named Kai. I… I have the address." I found the stack of mail and read it off to my mother. I couldn't live with Kai forever. Sure, I could feel this intimate relationship brewing between us, but given the situation, neither of us ever pursued more than stolen glances. I didn't think I had anything left in my body to create the concept of love. I was wrecked and scared. I slept with the guest room door locked, and the chair pushed against it, even though I knew, deep down, that Kai wouldn't hurt me.

"We will be there this week. We love you, Gia. Everything is going to be okay, now." My mother ended the call hurriedly. They were going to save me. They were going to save my baby. I looked down at my growing stomach and rubbed it.

"It's okay, my little butterfly."

———

I took a shower, began packing my belongings, and placed the envelope of money on the dresser. Kai had taken care of me for weeks, even knowing I couldn't pay him back. I left all the money he had given me and sat to write a letter I'd leave for him in a few days with some homemade Indian treats. I knew these words wouldn't be ones I'd be able to verbalize without crying, but it needed to be said.

Dear Kai,

Thank you for everything you have done for me when you owed me nothing. I will never understand how a human being could be as kind as you have been and provided a safe place for me until I could go home. I don't know if I believe in God anymore, but I do believe that my sister sent you to me to save me from the life that took hers. Not only did you save my life, you saved my child's. I will miss you and your fettuccini alfredo... I'm not sure which one more.

With love and gratitude,

Gia

. . .

I smiled and sealed the letter in an envelope before sliding it into my nightstand drawer. I then went to make a cup of chamomile tea. Turning the kettle on, I squinted as I looked into the shiny steel. Leaning closely, I held my breath as my lips parted. My sister was staring back at me. Her face was devoid of any emotion and then, a smile slowly grew against her lips. Not a gentle one but one filled with vengeance. Screaming, I turned and looked over my shoulder. No one was there. Letting out a long breath of air, I shook my head. I couldn't do this anymore.

Shaking, I walked to the wall-to-wall windows and hugged myself. It was so beautiful. The skyline was lit up, cars were still roaring through the streets, and I could see people, dressed in sparkly dresses and suits, walking along the sidewalk. It must be so wonderful to truly live. I swore to myself that I, too, would live. Just like the books I loved to read, my life was a book full of chapters. I couldn't rip it out and shred it, although, I'd prefer to. But I could use it to make the rest of my story beautiful and redemptive. My parents could help me with the baby; we could lie and say Raj died—that would be the only way having a child would be alright. Even if your husband was abusive, you were told to stay. He had to be dead.

Looking into the glass, my reflection was filled with hope. But that hope lasted only a moment as my reflection wasn't alone. *No, no, no.*

RAJ'S REFLECTION joined mine and I was paralyzed. I refused to look and see if it was my reality or my imagination.

"Hello, darling," he rasped as he dragged his fingernails down my arm. I held my breath as he turned my body slowly.

"Raj," I breathed out, my bottom lip quivering. He towered over me and took another step, forcing me to back into the glass wall.

"How did you know…" I mustered out as he brushed his index finger across my chin.

Dropping to his knees, he put both hands on my hips and drew my body closer. Kissing my stomach, he looked up at me. "How could you ever think to keep my son away from me?" His voice was eerily calm, as if we'd seen each other countless times this past week.

"How did you know?" I cried as he gripped my stomach and continued to brush his lips across my now exposed flesh.

Standing, he looked into my eyes. "Because my in-laws were kind enough to tell me." A sinister smile spread across his lips and it felt like he'd stabbed me.

My parents told him where I was. My parents had signed my death warrant. They weren't coming to save their daughter and grandchild. No, they were making sure they continued to receive money from my husband and keep their image intact with their community.

"Let's go home, wife." His hands curled around my wrist and he tugged, but I resisted. Digging my nails into his hand, I tried to pry his cold fingers off me, but it didn't make a difference. Instead, he slammed me against the glass with his teeth grinding together.

"Get your ass in my car or I'll take one of your boyfriend's butcher knives and leave you sliced up, waiting for him, you whore." Jerking my body as if I were a ragdoll, I knew Raj wasn't making a false threat.

"I know you want this baby, so you can sacrifice it to… Dakini." I gritted as I followed him, his hand gripping mine aggressively.

I knew not to yell or call out for help as we walked outside. I knew Raj would never rest until he won. He'd claim I was mentally ill, and he'd have my parents support to back his false accusations. The hearse was poorly parked, and I dreaded getting inside it. The scent inside overcame me and I leaned out and began vomiting onto the sidewalk. "Please, Raj. The smell," I pleaded.

He looked down at me with disgust before slamming the door shut."Dakini needs this child. She won't rest until she has a son. She's out for blood."

The putter of the engine turning on had my anxiety spike as I watched Kai's penthouse fade into the past. I'd never see him again. I couldn't jump out of the car because I knew the baby would be hurt. I began taking shallow, short breaths to not inhale the scent of rot and death.

"Why didn't your mother sacrifice you to her if she's been haunting you and the place you apparently call home?" I buckled my seatbelt, contemplating what my next step was going to be.

Raj looked over at me. "*She* started all of this. She's the one; she failed my father, so he had to end her." End her? The vagueness of the answer infuriated me.

"I wish she had died before having you." I knew I shouldn't have said that, but by the time the realization poured over me that this man had full control if I lived or died, he slammed his foot against the gas pedal. Before I knew it, the tires were crunching against the winding, gravel driveway. The dark, gray skies hung around the Rao Estate, and windowpanes were dangling as ivy climbed it like a snake slithers up a tree.

"I'm pregnant, Raj." I pleaded knowing my parents had already told him.

He got out and stormed past the front of the hearse before yanking my door open. I sucked in a long breath of fresh air as Raj grabbed my arm. His nails dug into my wrist while I instinctively dug my heels into the ground, attempting to slow him down.

But there was no hope. He was stronger than me, and he knew I wouldn't run again. This time I'd have no place to hide. He'd hunt me down and slaughter me.

"Raj, how can you sacrifice your own child? I will never let you hurt this baby." I was slapping at his hands as he opened the front door with my body arched to halt myself from entering the house from hell.

"But it isn't my child…is it, Amara?" He scoffed.

With one swift, shocking movement, he slapped me so hard that the ringing in my ears shook me to my core.

I felt waves of nausea course through me as exhaustion had my body folding in half. He was dragging me through the hall toward his personal morgue.

"No, Raj. No. Please. I'm not even full-term. I'm…"

The saltiness of my tears stung my tongue as I panted and begged, using my baby as a bargaining chip.

My words fell onto deaf ears as he opened the door, and the fluorescent lights blinded me. But just when I thought he was going to lay me across the cold, steel operating table, where God knows how many victims he claimed to be helping were strewn across, he pressed his thumb against a small pad. Just like that, a piece of the wall slowly opened.

My jaw dropped as panic replaced the nausea. "Raj, where are you taking me?"

He calmly pulled me through the frame and down a narrow, mostly broken set of wooden stairs. As soon as I saw the small bunker, I knew once the door shut behind me, I'd be lost forever.

Leaning down with all my might, I clamped my teeth into his wrist and bit until I tasted blood. He flung around, screeching, and pressed his hand against my head until I stopped and slipped backward. I watched his eyes widen as I collapsed and everything went dark.

THE WET SCENT of mud was pungent as I slowly opened my eyes, my head pounding. Coughing, I swallowed the minuscule amount of saliva lingering in my mouth to coat the dryness of my throat.

"Ugh," I groaned, clutching the back of my head, feeling my hair clump with moisture. There was a small lantern in the corner, cardboard boxes stacked by it, and nothing but mud and rocks composing the walls and ceiling.

I am underground.

My memory was hazy, but I remembered the whites of his eyes before collapsing. Turning my head slowly, I could hardly see well enough, but in the opposite corner, there was one gallon of water, what looked like some kind of food, and a bucket.

I wanted to scream and cry, but I couldn't—I was

numb from any emotion. My body was in agonizing pain, and tears rolled down my cheeks as I brushed my hand across my abdomen. "It's better this way, little butterfly. It's better if you don't grow anymore," I whispered with both my eyes and nose dripping. I laid there helpless for what felt like an eternity. Raj needed this baby for his superstition-based psychosis. He was probably just making a point by throwing me in here.

Pressing my hands into the dirt, I pushed myself upward. I hated small spaces, and once I stood, the panic of it all sank in. My head gazed the ceiling. "No, no…" I moved to the steel door that locked me in and began screaming at the top of my lungs.

"Raj! Please! Help! Raj!" I kept calling out while thrashing my aching hands against the cold, unforgiving steel until my skin grew raw. I heard something in between my cries.

Clank, clank, clank.

It was the same noise I'd hear when sleeping in our bedroom, but this time, it was louder. It was closer.

My heart slowed as I dragged my hands off the door and turned. "Hello?" I managed to whisper, my voice hoarse.

Another wave of nausea grew inside me. "Hello?"

Dropping to my knees, there was a small vent. "Hello!" I shouted into the cracks. Jolting upright, I raced to grab the lantern and brought it back, collapsing onto the floor to see inside.

It was another bunker.

That meant there had to be another person in there.

"Amara!" I cried out. "Amara, sister, please." I sobbed as my voice echoed.

"Shh… he will hear." It was a soft voice, but distant. It was my sister. I sucked in a breath of air as I pressed my face against the small metal bars.

My sister was alive; she was being held captive all this time. I didn't want to admit it, but my heart felt comfort and a blanket of peace wrapped around my body knowing I wasn't alone.

"I'm going to get us out. I'm going to get us out," I repeated as the metal dug into my cheek. "Say something, my sister." I sniffled.

"Don't talk so much. He can hear…" I could barely hear her. It must be a longer, more narrow space below.

"Are you chained?" It all started to piece together. These spaces had to connect to the ventilation, and the clanking was…

"What's your name?"

I pushed myself up, my eyes wide. "Amara… what…" I stammered. "It's me."

Her voice was completely different. It was innocent and young.

"I'm Gia. Who… Amara, who is that?"

"I'm me. I'm me." She giggled.

"Hi… the lady with you… is that your mama?"

"No, no… this isn't Mama."

My eyes stung, my lips were dry, and my entire body ached. There was pounding in the back of my head that caused my ears to ring.

"Shh… he's going to hear you," the woman repeated as the chains jingled. Just as I was about to continue to ask questions, not caring if Raj heard me or not, a door opened.

But it wasn't mine.

"Food!" the sweet voice below cried out.

"Raj! You monster!" I screamed. "You're not a man; you're a coward. A pathetic coward."

"No, no… please no!" the woman pleaded as the chains rattled. Jerking back, I slapped my hands across my mouth as the little girl began to cry.

"No, don't take food away!"

"That is on you, Gia. Shut your mouth," Raj called out from below.

A door slammed, and the woman and little girl began to cry. The woman was comforting her. I didn't have to see them to know that.

What had I done?

Worst of all, what had Raj done, and what more was he going to do?

MY BODY WAS SHAKING, but I didn't feel the movement. I had pulled my knees to my chest and stared at the flickering lantern. Hunger, nausea, and sheer exhaustion accumulated inside me, but I didn't fixate on any of it. The woman had to be my sister. My sister and a little girl that wasn't her daughter were apparently right below me. How long had they been there? The little girl hadn't stopped sobbing, probably from pangs of hunger because of me.

"Is that your daughter?" I whispered. I had to know who she was.

"No," she said.

"Who is she, then?"

"A lost little girl. Now, shh… or he will hear you." The chains clamored. Raj went to their bunker through another entrance, so there may be no way for me to ever see them. I looked at the small vent-like space.

Defeat had already wrapped itself around me as I thought of the ridiculous ways I'd go down there and save them and myself. I'd save my child and...

Just as I dreamed of ways to survive, the door slid sideways. My husband was standing in the doorframe, his eyes heavy, the bags underneath deepened and darker.

"Dakini has been torturing me. Did you know that? She's haunting me, moving things in the house and..." He waved his hands wildly as he spoke rapidly.

"This is for you." He placed a plate down in front of me. "You need to start eating meat. The iron will help the baby."

The sudden shift was startling, and was more terrifying than the frantic trance he was in moments ago.

I had never consumed meat in my entire life. Staring down at the plate, there was breaded chicken or maybe steak? There wasn't anything else.

"I don't, Raj. You know I don't eat meat." I almost laughed at the way I spoke to him. A distraught wife simply telling her husband she doesn't like what he's brought.

Raj looked at me, then walked toward the bucket. "You haven't urinated yet. Just remember, you're not hurting me… you're only hurting our child and your-self. This is what you're going to eat, and if not, you both can die."

He spun around on his heels and walked back to the steel door that had automatically shut when he entered. Lifting his right thumb, he pressed it against the small pad, and the door opened. The rest of the house hadn't left the seventies, but the bunker door resembled something from the future.

He cared more about keeping us caged than the way he lived.

Staring at the meat, I swallowed the lump in my throat. There wasn't a fork or knife. I brushed my finger against it as the odor of it wafted into my nose and I gagged. Pushing it to the side, my stomach turned, and I crawled over to the bucket. Choking on my own vomit, I cried as stomach acid burned my esophagus.

"Please God, help me." The vomiting didn't stop and eventually, my body gave out. I fell asleep clutching onto the plastic bucket for dear life. I wasn't going to survive.

"Here," a harsh voice awoke me from my sleep. I was instantly light-headed as soon as I opened my eyes.

He was wearing scrubs, and from the scent of the nauseating Irish Spring soap, I knew the bastard had enjoyed a nice, hot shower.

"What is it?" I looked at the contents in front of me on the plate.

"It's a hash brown mix." My stomach was grumbling, and I knew as much as starving to death sounded appealing, given my situation, I couldn't bear the guilt of knowing I didn't at least try to save the life growing inside me.

Nodding, I looked over at the plate from the day before. The meat was left untouched and would probably become my dinner if I didn't accept whatever strange breakfast was being shoved in front of me.

"Thank you," I forced out as he crossed his arms and watched me intently.

"Eat. Or do you not care about the baby?" He said it so matter-of-factly.

I had to bite back the laughter brewing inside me at the sheer irony. He had his pregnant wife caged with his first wife and a little unknown child.

Lifting the spoon, I shoved some of the mix into my mouth.

It wasn't bad.

"Is this…"

"Chicken. It's high in protein, and you need that. The *baby* needs that." I nodded and took a bite. Who knew he could actually cook and season food properly.

I was eating better here than I ever did while free.

Free. What a ridiculous word to use in regards to my life in general. Had I ever truly been free? Back in India, I was repressed and taught to believe women were inferior. Here, it was the same thing, but now instead of my parents holding the control, my husband was.

Raj watched me shovel the food into my mouth rapidly. A small smile grew on his face.

"What?" I said as some of the potato crumbled out of my mouth.

Brushing his hand across his jawline, he tilted his head...

"If the sacrifice works, we will have another baby together. We will build our family, finally. We will have peace." I was sitting on the cold floor eating a plate of food as if I was a chained dog, and this man was planning our family in his delusional mind.

"I'm not your family, Raj. I'm nothing to you, because the truth is, my sister isn't dead, is she?" I forced myself to my feet and looked up at him. "You and I aren't married." Pointing down, I shook my head. "My sister has been here all along, hasn't she? Being held in a bunker, chained up and tortured for how long?" My voice shook with each word.

Raj looked at me with confusion. "Oh, my darling wife… you have truly lost your mind. Your sister died. She is gone, much to my despair, as you know. I deeply, truly loved her. There will never be someone as perfect as she was. But she couldn't give me the sacrifice. Without the sacrifice, I'll never live the life I deserve."

"No… no…" I spewed while stepping back from him. Dropping to my knees and hovering over the vent, I screeched inside. "Hello, talk to me!" I begged they'd respond. I needed them to respond. I needed them to prove that Raj wasn't right.

Cold hands gripped my arms from behind as my body flailed.

"No! They are there. Take me there… now!" I bashed my hands against the hard dirt floor embedded with rocks.

Raj used more force to lift me and slammed my back against the wall. Clenching my eyes shut, the pain was excruciating.

His hands tightened around my wrists as he crashed them above my head. "Stop it! I can't keep doing this. You need to stop! You came back to me and just…be back *with* me." His voice was full of something I'd never heard before.

Vulnerability.

His breath was cold against my face as he dropped

his head and pressed it against mine. "I wish she were trapped in one place, because instead, she's... everywhere. You're everywhere."

I WOKE up with my stomach tumbling. It wasn't the nausea from the baby; no, this was nausea from the meal I ate not settling well inside me. Hurrying over to the dirtied bucket, I gagged at the odor from my own bodily fluids and vomited. My ribs ached from each intense movement as I clutched myself in agony. Tossing my head back, I cried out, "Help me." I felt dizzy, and my mind didn't feel like my own.

"Don't let her die..." a hushed whisper brushed against my ear.

Flinging around, I scooted back and pressed myself against the wall.

Looking around wildly, my body shook. I stared at the stacks of cardboard boxes on the opposing wall.

Perhaps the dehydration, lack of nutrition, or poor

sleep were finally catching up to me. Perhaps I'd been delirious all along.

I burst into laughter and couldn't stop. My laughter echoed against the four tight walls. I was putting myself through this torture. I didn't need to be here. I had to.

"What a beautiful sound…" a little voice called out.

I sucked in a breath and slapped my hands over my mouth.

Hunching over the small vent, I pressed my face against it and peered down.

It was just dirt. There were no signs of anything. If Amara and a little girl were chained down there all this time, wouldn't there be something?

Anything.

Looking up, I crawled on all fours to the boxes. Some of them were opened, while others were taped repeatedly in all directions with no way to open them —especially since I didn't have something sharp to cut through. If I had something to cut through them, I'd have prioritized cutting through my husband's flesh.

Prying the top off, I dug through and saw endless stacks of faded newspapers. Most were dated decades ago.

I scanned through multiple pages of each set in hopes to find some kind of information that gave reasoning of why these would be hoarded away. The dates were scattered, and when I got to the bottom of the first box, I froze.

Swallowing, my heart began to race as I tugged it out.

RECLUSE, ERRATIC, AND WEALTHY MR. RAO ASSUMED TO BE DEAD

Mr. Amir Rao was a man of few words but filled with anger that kept most of the city away. The Rao family immigrated from India and kept to themselves. Known to be surviving off generational wealth, no one truly got through the walls of the anchorite cliffside mansion. According to officers, a car was found floating in the ocean, and it is believed to be an attempted murder-suicide.

A woman was found unconscious in the home, and stated she was the owner and that her husband had tried to kill her, but she jumped out of the moving vehicle and made her way back inside her home. Her son, Dr. Raj Rao, was also found chained in a bunker, which he claims his father did before dragging his mother out in the car. Dr. Rao claims he was checking in on his family, who were not returning his calls, when the situation grew violent and deadly. He will be caring for his now paralyzed mother and residing in the Rao Estate, which locals have long referred to as a haunted house. Claims of cries and shadows have long been whispered about from those who have managed to enter for repairs or teenagers who were acting on a dare.

Dr. Raj Rao retired from his position back in Boston and remains at home with his mother.

Raj's parents didn't die in a car accident? His father tried to kill his mother? My breathing hitched as I re-read the words. Raj wasn't even a practicing doctor, anymore. Where was he getting all of these bodies? My hands shook as I took everything in.

I could hear movement from outside the door.

Shoving the papers inside the box, I held my breath before the door slid open. But it wasn't Raj; it was Kali ma—the woman from the small oceanside cave.

She had a bright red bhindi in the center of her forehead and her deep brown eyes were heavily lined in smudged eyeliner.

"You are with-child." The long orange gown fell over her thin frame as she glided in.

I clutched my growing stomach and shook as her presence made the room feel colder.

Dropping to the ground, she pushed aside the hair from my face and gripped my chin between her index finger and thumb.

"You've been burdened," she rasped, the scent of herbs and incense emitting off of her.

"Please save me. Call the police. I think he has my sister. I think he has a little girl."

Kali ma slammed her finger against my lips. "Sweet child, you will be killed after this baby is born. If the baby is lucky, so will she." Running her hands across my stomach, she closed her eyes and took a deep breath. "No one can help you. No one. Just think, she couldn't even save you."

She sat in front of me crossing her legs as the whites of her eyes illuminated by the small lantern in her hands.

She started chanting in a language I'd never heard. My heart raced rapidly as the papers began to flutter wildly.

"Please stop!" I screamed. Kali ma didn't care as her eyes began rolling and her thin lips roared out words.

Dakini. Dakini. Dakini.

And finally, I understood a bit of what she said.

Dakini, the baby is yours. The sacrifice will be done soon.

I began screaming but it didn't matter because the walls caged my pain in. Before I knew it, I collapsed.

———

The days blended into one. Raj would come in once a day and bring the same plate of some kind of hash brown and chicken mix. He finally emptied the bucket and, for some reason, my face flooded in embarrassment as if I were living like this by choice.

I cried, I pleaded, I bargained, but nothing worked. I was going to die here, and if Kali ma was truly right, so would this baby.

But even if this child was a boy, wouldn't Raj sacrifice him to settle the score with the spirit he thought had cursed his family?

I lifted another box and had been clawing at it, and finally, I broke through the tape.

It was filled with random items that made no sense. I tried calling out to the voices below, assuming someone was there. But I no longer heard the little girl's voice, or the woman's.

Tugging out a worn leather journal, I opened it and instantly recognized the handwriting.

Amara's.

I flipped through the pages, knowing if Raj saw me with it, he'd rip it away. I dragged my finger down her beautiful cursive, but as I turned each page, her handwriting got worse.

"Save her," a whisper brushed against my neck as I flung around.

"Amara," I choked out. She was once pregnant here… The fear and pain she must have felt had to have been even worse for her—she was the gentler one of us.

Looking down at the page, I began to read familiar words.

I was close to escaping, but then I heard the voice I'd hear through the vents at the late hours of night when sweat trickled down my temples and my body ached from Raj thrashing me around for denying being intimate with him. He'd force himself on me, of course. Every day things happened in this house. Splatters of blood appeared, shadows standing out of the shower glass. Footsteps echoing and whispers into my ear. I knew it was two different voices. I didn't know, either. But then, I followed Raj one day. I watched him enter a door on the side. I knew someone was there. So, when he drove away in his hearse, I went to the door and pried it open.

I fell back because she was right there. I saw the look of fear in her eyes when I opened the side door that was covered in the thick greenery. I saw the way she had to be my age, but because of how starved she was, could have passed for a teenager. I asked her who she was, but she didn't answer. She didn't open her lips. Until I said that I'd get us help. All she had to do was come with me. But her eyes widened, and she said, "Shh, he will hear you." Then she retreated into the darkness. She pleaded with me to shut her door and leave her be.

So I did. I ran as fast as I could. I went inside to grab the small bag I'd packed away. I went to see Mami. Everything she told me the night before made me realize I had to have the courage to leave. Finally leave.

I would get her help.

Mami told me how she wasn't Raj's mother. No, she was his nanny. She had witnessed the horrors these walls clung to.

She had witnessed Raj's father chaining the girl away. She had witnessed him murdering his wife and then, so did Raj.

Raj saw it all. He saw his father slaughter his mother because she gave birth to a girl. His father, a delusional misogynist, was convinced a daughter would bring bad fortune to the family. But then, the true bad fortune was what happened after Raj's mother died.

I had not noticed that I was crying as loudly as I was until I heard the little girl shout from below, "He's coming!" Slamming the journal shut, I stuffed it into the box before sliding the other on top. Huddling into the corner, I pretended to be asleep, and before I knew it, the door opened.

"Food. You need to eat," Raj said aggressively as he grabbed the stacked plates and shoved them into an empty bucket he brought in.

It was the same thing every single day. Every time I ate the food, it made me feel sick, but it also prevented me from vomiting. So, I ate it.

"Shouldn't I be taking vitamins or eating a more…"

Raj stood with his arms crossed, eyeing me. His frown lifted into a smile. "This child is strong enough without all that artificial bullshit. Once he's here, I'll be free from the misfortune every Rao man has suffered at the hands of disgruntled, ungrateful women."

"How is a baby boy going to magically save you all from what I'm assuming is a lot of blood on all your hands?"

Raj pushed off the wall and grew closer to me. What was I thinking?

"That woman… my mother knew too much."

Letting out a dry laugh, I eyed him up and down. "Mami wasn't your mother." I was being irrational; I knew I couldn't let him know how much I knew. It was irresponsible.

But the rage inside wouldn't let me stop. I couldn't let him live peacefully while he had me caged. Jolting up, I flung my fists into his chest, which did nothing but anger him more.

Tilting his head slightly, he clenched his hands around my flailing wrists and dragged me with ease outside the room. As soon as we were inside the icy in-home morgue, I knew this was my chance to run.

I had to run.

Clamping my teeth down into his flesh, he screamed but I didn't let go. Not even when the taste of iron from his blood painted my tongue.

Instead, he tugged me harder and turned on the sink. Slamming my face into it as it filled, I shrieked and fought back, but the strength in my body wasn't there. He looped his hand into my hair, providing an extra painful grip as he crushed my jaw into the dirtied steel and let the water pool over my face. Gurgling on the water, I couldn't scream anymore. I clenched my eyes shut as I dug my nails into his hands.

He was drowning me. Just as the world around me started to close in, I opened my eyes slowly and saw her face in front of me.

My sister.

"Fight. Fight for me. Fight for her." I could hear her words clearer than the sound of my own sobbing and choking.

Reaching up for his hands, I dug my jagged nails deep into his skin until I heard him shriek from the pain.

"Bitch!" He released me for just enough time that I flung around and stabbed him with my fingers as hard as I could in his eyes before running towards the door.

He was curled on the ground, calling out in agony, but once I thought I had won, luck reminded me that there was no winning with a monster. The door required Raj's fingerprint. He stood and brushed his hands against his eyes as I ran to grab a surgical tool. Waving it wildly, I began to threaten him.

"Just tell me who the people in the other bunker are? Who?" I screeched, saliva dripping from my mouth while rage rampaged through me.

Raj dropped his shoulders and sighed. "Gia, please. I need you to listen to me. Just listen to me." He held his hands up as if he were waving a white flag.

Trembling, I pressed my back against the steel door blocking me from the main house and kept the blade up as steady as my hands would allow.

"Get me out of here. Now," I hissed at him, but truly, I didn't know where I was going with this. I didn't know what I was doing.

Raj nodded with sadness in his eyes. "Gia, I didn't want to be like this. I didn't. I... know this has all gotten so out of fucking control. I will let us both out, but I need you to listen to me and believe what I have to say. Gia, your dad is not doing well. I don't want to have to use him as blackmail, but it's all I have to convince you to just stop thinking we are on opposing teams."

I was on the cusp of a mental breakdown, or perhaps I was already muddled into one. My stomach started to cramp as if knives were slicing through my ribs.

"Ah!" I cried out, clutching my sides as my long, damp hair dangled in front of my eyes. I felt a sharp pain.

"Darling..." Raj's eyes dropped down as I looked back at him. Following his line of vision, I knew what he was seeing because I could feel it.

I could feel the blood trickling out of me and crafting a river against my leg.

Dropping down to my knees, my head was far too light for me to stand much longer. I was giving out and now, I had failed my parents, my sister, my unborn child, and most of all, I had failed myself.

This was it.

I was dying.

Looking at Raj, my lips quivered. "Raj... please help my parents. Please keep Papa alive. Please." Falling face forward, I could feel the air between the ground and my face. I could hear Raj shout my name and lunge forward.

But he was too late…

I KNEW I had made a grave mistake. I knew that what I had done was punishable by death. Back in India, I'd have been laid on the sticks and lit up with a match. I would have been shunned for going against my husband. But I was desperate. I needed to get him to stop. He was meticulously tracking my cycle. He was forcing himself on me every night of my fertile window, even though I cried in agony.

I needed to get pregnant, and I prayed every single day. I even placed each of Mama's goddess statues neatly and lit the incense and candles by them. I chanted the mantras she told me about before I left. She knew I needed to give Raj a son soon. There was this pressure-filled cloud hovering over my head as I stressed about growing a family when I didn't even feel like Raj was mine.

Unlike my little sister, Gia, I was obedient. I knew that this was my duty—not only to my husband, but to my parents. It was our duty, as women, to bridge gaps, not make them. I felt like my efforts were well received by Raj. I made him hot, delectable meals and washed his clothes. I tidied up as best as I could, although the house truly needed professional assistance. But I wasn't going to complain about the enormous three-story, ocean-side estate. I came from a one-bedroom, so-called house. Gia and I slept on a broken mattress in the kitchen.

Oh, Gia.

I sank into the library and looked at all the books lining the shelves. She'd have loved this so much. My little butterfly was more so my little bookworm. She loved to read more than anyone I knew. Guilt panged me as I thought about how she must have been waiting for a personalized letter detailing all my American adventures and experiences. But Raj hovered over my shoulder when I wrote the occasional letter to my parents. I lied in most of them, keeping them formal. I hoped it would provide them some kind of reassurance that their elder daughter was thriving, and they could rest and only worry about their wild child, which was always my younger sister. I couldn't help but laugh and wipe the tears away. Brushing my hand against my swollen stomach, I knew she'd be a girl.

I knew deep down inside this baby wasn't a boy.

In any other life, I'd have been so thrilled. I had always wanted a baby girl, but I was always told that sons were superior. A daughter would leave me behind once married. A daughter was no longer ours once her last name changed. It was silly, considering a daughter is never ours, not even as we cradle her in our arms. We look down at her with knowing eyes that she is his. He is out there in the world, and one day will marry her and she will obey him and his parents. She will become theirs. She was always theirs.

But I didn't believe that. A daughter cares and feels the connection to her parents in a way that causes both pain and joy. A daughter doesn't wish to be separated or forced to focus solely on her husband's family. No, she is forced to do so. Because that is the truest, most selfless form of love. When a daughter has to pretend her love for her own is not as important as the love for the ones she's been forced to be with.

Gia, my Gia. She was born to the wrong family, the wrong culture, the wrong world. She tried to be the way that was expected, but no, she wasn't meant to.

I could see her running off into the sunset with some tall, broody American man with hair the color of sand. I could see her refusing to have children, and instead, insist on pursuing an education we'd never been allowed to have. Sure, much of India had modernized, but arranged marriages still held the top way any of us were getting married. It didn't matter how educated, how developed, or how determined. Ultimately, our parents knew best. But I had a feeling Gia would put up a good fight. And now, looking around at my new life, I was envious of her more than ever. I wondered how she would have handled my story.

———

There was always something off in this house. The way the shadowy figures would dance behind the stilled curtains or the way I'd hear a woman's voice brush against my neck, pleading with me to save 'her'. On the rare chance I had garnered enough courage to call Ma, I told her. I told her about the way I feel a force—a dark one at that—that seemingly fell over me and made it feel harder to breathe or move.

I told her how I'd see random footprints on a freshly mopped floor leading me to the end of the hall-way. I'd hear a woman sobbing in Mami's room that wasn't her. My mother said that every home had spirits that weren't at rest. Often times, it was relatives who may have passed and had more to say, or ancestors filled with disappointment. It was our duty to pray for their souls to rest, and then to cleanse our home for our living, breathing family to thrive in.

But I tried and I prayed. I did everything I could. Raj was growing more and more hostile with every negative pregnancy test. The voice of the distraught woman pleading with me to save 'her' grew louder and louder.

He told me I was going insane. And part of me began to believe him. Didn't those with severe psychosis claim they weren't mentally unstable?

What if I was falling ill here?

But then, I met him, and everything changed. Kai was the light I so desperately sought out. When I was with him, I didn't hear the voices, I didn't see the shadows. I was alive. I ran away from Raj. Months of him abusing me was more than I could handle. We'd go out to Kai's restaurant and pretend we were a happily married couple, but I think Kai could see past the veil of lies.

The day I showed up to his restaurant was the start of something completely new. He saved me. We spent two months together. Two months of bliss and love that were worth an entire lifetime. But then I became comfortable, and when Kai worked, I'd go out and wander the city streets.

Someone told Raj they had seen me. Someone led

him to corner me outside of a coffee shop and drag me back to my hell. Kai didn't come for me.

He never came for me.

Raj forced himself on me that night, and it was the most painful thing my body had gone through. I lied to him and said I was at a women's shelter, and he believed my lies. I was well-fed and well dressed, so he knew I wasn't on the streets. I also knew he'd murder Kai if he found out. I had also realized that Kai loved me and I loved him. I didn't even know what love was, but that's what it felt like in the brief time I was with Kai. But ultimately, love is simply a word… a meaningless word. Looking back, I couldn't have been more wrong. I had become exactly what my mother had warned me about—a married woman who throws herself on a man and sleeps with him, a whore. We run so far from our parents' beliefs but maybe that is the issue. If I had listened to my mother, I wouldn't be living in even more paralyzing fear.

I was pregnant.

And it wasn't Raj's child.

MY PAPA WAS a calm man compared to many of the fathers I knew in my village. My mother was the one who was vile and abusive toward me. She was enamored by beautiful Amara. She knew Amara would be the one who'd listen to everything they'd tell her to do. What someone else considers abnormal is completely normal to the next person. That's the only way I could justify so much of this world. *My world.*

I laid in bed—our bed—next to my husband. He sat me down, pushing a loaded gun into my stomach, and looked into my eyes. "If you ever try to run again or do anything that is other than what you are intended to do, which is be my wife and give birth to this child, then I will make sure I hunt you down like the wild animal you are behaving like and then, I will chop your body up and place it in a box and personally fly it home to your parents."

I missed being caged inside the bunker; I was safer there than here. But I knew that Raj wasn't just threatening me, he was warning me. If I ran, then I would not only lose my life and my parents' lives, but my child's.

I stared at the ceiling and watched as the rickety fan slowly sliced through the air. My body was covered in a glaze of sweat, even though Raj forced me to slide into the cold tub and bathe me. His eyes lit up when he saw the curve of my growing stomach. He almost looked… human?

"Gia." A voice startled me as I looked to the side. The curtain twirled, even though the window was closed. It had to be the air from the fan, I reasoned.

"Gia, please…" she whispered. A shadow fell onto the floor and grew closer. Gripping the blanket, I tugged it under my chin and shook my head. No, please, no. I couldn't do this.

"Gia, come… come with me." What felt like cold fingers brushed against my arm. Blowing out a breath of air, I looked over at Raj before sliding out. I didn't see the shadow, but I felt a shift in air around me, guiding me. I gripped the banister and tip-toed down the winding stairwell, avoiding the areas I knew would creak loudly. I kept walking as if my body wasn't my own and saw the door to the morgue was wide open. I wanted to glance over my shoulder, but I couldn't. My body was in a trance-like state, so I continued to follow the force around me and into the morgue. My lips parted as the second door to the bunker was opened. I didn't want to go in, but I watched my feet move forward.

I was being pulled forward.

Walking into the space I was held in, I feared the door would close behind me, but my body wouldn't allow me to stop. The cardboard boxes stacked in the corner began to fall over and crashed onto the floor. My heart raced as I looked up, wondering when I'd hear Raj's feet storming down the stairs, but the silence fluttered around me while the space felt congested as if I weren't alone.

Amara's journal slammed to the ground and, as if a storm were rolling through the house, pages fluttered rapidly. Wrapping my arms around myself, I clenched my eyes shut as gusts of cold air slapped against my body and the bunker.

Multiple shrill screams—those of women—pierced through my ears, leaving a ringing, and then…

Everything stilled.

My body was coated in a cold sweat as my feet moved forward, and I bent over. Lifting the journal in my hands it was opened to a stained page.

He's going to kill me. I know he will. He knows this baby is a girl, and she'll be here any day now. Rage has filled him in a way I didn't think was possible. He dragged me into the morgue and laid me on the table. I swore he was about to slice me open and tear the baby out, but instead, he performed an ultrasound. He saw it was a girl. The way he slammed things around the room had me lying there, paralyzed in fear that if I even exhaled he'd kill me. And her. If he was this upset about the baby being a girl, I wondered how upset he'd be knowing it wasn't his. I knew I had to leave, or I'd end up just like his mother. Raj was a monster created from his youth.

Mami told me everything. Well, she tried. After what Raj did to her tongue, I knew she'd never speak the same again. He took scissors to her tongue, kitchen shears, and cut it as a warning. The slur in her words wasn't from the paralysis; it was from Raj. It all had been from Raj. He was a monster.

Looking down at my round belly, tears streamed down my cheeks. I'm sorry that he's going to kill you, but what kind of life is this to live? What I wonder is if the girl that Raj's dad once chained up ever made it out? Who was she? Was she Mami's daughter. Where was she now? Or… was she lucky enough to die?

We could die together, baby girl. We'd be together somewhere better than here.

. . .

Amara had the baby. The cold broke away from me as I stood in the bunker and walked forward. Kneeling, I looked through the vent. "Hello," I rasped. My voice echoed with nothing in return. What girl did Raj's dad chain up? What was Raj's childhood like that made him into what he was to this capacity? Why did these words feel so familiar?

Tears fell from my eyes as the metallic taste lingering in my mouth reminded me of the life growing inside me and how, before I knew it… she may have the same fate my niece had. I threw the journal down into the boxes full of books and saved newspapers. Turning around, I walked to the back door and opened it. The ocean waves were crashing against the boulder and splatters of a light drizzle pelted down on me.

I cried as I cradled my stomach and looked at the ocean. We were raised to believe in karma. What comes around, goes around. But what had I ever done in my life that would lead me here? What did my sister's baby girl do that had her killed? I felt more alone than ever, even though a life was growing inside me. Pregnancy can do that to you, though—isolate you even more because now you have two lives to think about instead of one.

I went inside with my nightgown drenched in a combination of rain and sweat. I lifted the phone and dialed my parents' number. Sniffling, I waited until my father picked up.

But I didn't speak. I had too many words and none at all for the people who brought me into this world and threw me into the arms of danger.

"Beta." He knew I was in trouble. He knew he signed over his daughter, no, his daughters lives, and for what? Societal expectation? Religious beliefs? Monetary relief and gain?

My breathing hitched. "Papa, I'm pregnant with a baby girl." I just needed him to know. I wasn't even sure, but deep down, I knew it. I needed someone else in this world to know about this little girl, because there was more likelihood that the baby and I wouldn't make it. I was thankful it wasn't my mother answering the phone, considering she led Raj to me. She baited me and tricked me into thinking they'd save me.

I couldn't think of that in this moment. The grim reaper was coming for me. When this baby was born, that would be the end of both our lives.

"Gia…" my father cried. In my entire life, I'd never heard my father cry. I was convinced he was incapable. It was probably drilled into his head that boys don't cry, and men definitely do not, either.

"Run away," he hissed into the phone.

Clutching the receiver, and sobbing as silently as I could, I shook my head. "There's nowhere to run, Papa. There's no home to run to. There's…"

"I know, Gia. I know."

Sniffling, I couldn't believe this. My own father knew I was going to die soon. That his grandchild, his second grandchild, was about to die, too. Yet, there he was… helpless or choosing not to help.

Looking down, I brushed my hand on the stomach I didn't recognize. "I'm scared to die, Papa."

I wanted to yell at him, to beg him to save me, but I think we both had accepted none of that was possible anymore. It was too late. Time had run out. In just a few short months, I would give birth, and then this child would be sacrificed to Dakini.

"Death is a part of life, Gia. You will be reborn… I hope to a better father, one who could protect you."

Letting out a saddened laugh, I wiped the tears from under my eyes. "In my next life, I want to be born as a man. That would be the greatest gift of them all."

I WAS CLUTCHING the worn book filled with Indian folklore about Dakini. Tracing my fingers against the image of the goddess holding sliced male heads, I continued to read the faded words. A woman who dies during childbirth or pregnancy due to trauma inflicted on her will resurface and torment until she seeks revenge. She can come back as any form.

Brushing my hand across my tired scowl, I couldn't differentiate between reality and what my mind was doing. I wasn't superstitious like everyone in my village; I didn't believe that something supernatural could wreak havoc on our lives. But now, I did. If my dead sister was a tormented spirit, then she must have died during childbirth or pregnancy. If her child died, too, then she was seeking revenge.

Closing my eyes, I needed answers. I hadn't

accepted that death was the answer. I knew running away would mean Raj would chain me up until this baby was born, and then he'd slaughter me. I knew I had to outsmart him. I had to think like a man to beat him. Drifting off, I hoped I could escape my reality with my dreams.

———

I could feel sharp fingernails rake across my stomach. I could feel the cold presence towering over me. "Ladka," the voice whispered. *Boy.*

"Save them," she rasped. Opening my eyes, I flung upward, gasping for air.

It was a nightmare. I blew out a breath and reached for the matchbox before striking one against the pad. Watching the flame flicker, I lit the candlestick that was almost completely melted. I lifted it and pushed the blanket off my belly.

My eyes widened as I saw the red nail marks. Tilting my head, my lips parted. It wasn't just scratches. No, it was two butterflies drawn into my flesh that was splattered with stretch marks.

Amara.

Looking around, I didn't feel her. I didn't feel the way I did when I knew my sister was alive. We weren't twins, but we were one in so many ways.

"Who? Save who?" I cried out as a book dropped off the bookshelf and its pages fluttered.

Racing to it, I dropped to the ground and looked at the one word highlighted.

Basement.

The bunker? There had to be a side door to get to the bunker below the one I was kept in.

Jumping up, I grabbed an old knit cardigan that must have been Mami's and draped it over myself.

Glancing over my shoulder, I pushed my feet into the dirtied rainboots and carefully unlocked the front door. A gust of cold sea air slapped against me as I gripped the cardigan together.

Dragging my feet through the moist gravel, I looked around as the wind howled. I had been terrified to leave this house. The one time I finally did landed me in a small space, relieving myself in a bucket and wishing for death.

I thought about Kai for a brief moment. He didn't care enough to come for me, to check in. But then I remembered…

The note. I had written that I was leaving for India, that my parents were coming for me. He must have thought I had left. My feet slid across the slick mud and gravel mixture as I walked around and patted the worn stone of the house. I didn't see any doors. Glancing around wildly, with only the moonlight shining down on me, I could taste the saltiness in the air from the ocean crashing just steps away.

Small drops fell on my face. Looking up, I could see darker clouds looming in the distance. A storm was coming.

My heart began to race. Raj always woke up when thunder crackled. The rain began to fall faster, and I picked up my pace, brushing my hands across the siding of the house. I was losing hope as the rain fell harder and the thin flower nightgown I was wearing clung to my body.

But just as I began to turn around, the air grew colder around me. Someone was here.

Swallowing I looked down and could see a shadow covering my body. My spine straightened.

Raj.

Turning around slowly, I exhaled with relief no one was there. As soon as I turned back around a blanket of cold gripped around me as the shadow grew. Someone was here, but it wasn't anyone I could see. Sucking in a breath of air I shuddered.

I gripped the side of the house as the rubber of the boots began to slosh against the wet mud. I was growing exhausted as my eyes blurred from the rain catching on my lashes and my mind pleaded for sleep.

"Ah." My arms shot out to steady myself as I

missed my footing. Nails dug into my arms, lifting me back to my feet just as I began to fall.

"Below," her voice crooned in my ear followed by an icy chill. It wasn't Amara's voice. No, it was someone else's. An older woman, perhaps?

"I don't see anything. I can't find a door. I..." I cried out.

I gripped my hips as the pain of my growing belly was weighing more and more on my knees. The rubber sole of my boot slapped against something. Stomping once more in the same spot, my eyes widened as I dropped down and patted the metal handle.

"Bastard." There was a layer of mud, water, and rocks scattered over it, and the rain slanted harder as I tugged. Groaning out loudly, I jerked the handle backward as hard as I could until I fell straight back.

It didn't even budge. My palms were aching from the measly attempt. It was locked. There was no way Raj would be reckless. But I couldn't give up. Looking around, I pleaded with the universe, pleaded with her to hear me and help me.

"I can't do this alone." I squatted and pulled with as much force as I could. I hadn't realized I was biting my tongue as I tugged until I could taste blood.

Cold air wrapped around my hands, and I closed my eyes.

She was here. Whoever she was, she was here. And I wasn't afraid.

Screaming out, I pulled the metal handle until finally, the small, hidden door opened.

Relief and anxiety pooled inside me as I looked down. I could see a small light flickering, and as I pushed the door up, my heart raced faster. There was a narrow rope ladder leading down.

"Hello?" My throat was dry and scaly, so the word came out hoarse.

Silence.

Looking over my shoulder, I didn't feel the cold air around me. I was alone. Gripping the edge of the entrance, I turned my body slowly and wiggled my foot until I could feel the first step. It was wobbling as soon as my weight landed on it. Grabbing onto the side, I held my breath as I descended into the darkness.

I SHUDDERED as soon as my feet hit the ground. The air was frigid, and a musky odor clung around.

Turning slowly, my heart sank.

No one was there. It was a large space with one flickering lantern. The dirt floors had puddles of water, and looking up, I realized it was because the makeshift ceiling was leaking in patches.

Putting one foot in front of the other, I held my breath as I heard voices. Glancing over my shoulder, I could see the small entrance still open. Raj had to be asleep still because if he was awake, he'd have most definitely dragged me out of here and locked me away. The drops of water dissolved into the dirt as the rain continued to seep in. "Hello?" I whispered while I looked around, trying to see where the distant voices were coming from. I didn't see a door.

"Hello, there," a hushed whisper behind me sent chills up my spine as I slowly turned around.

A little girl. Her eyes were the most beautiful, brilliant shade of blue. Her long black hair was tousled over her shoulders. In one hand, she was dangling a small worn teddy bear. Her small frame was covered in a pale pink nightgown. For the first time in a very long time, I felt a blanket of warmth cover my body. Dropping down to my knees, I let out a small laugh as tears fell from my eyes. Reaching my hand out, I brushed her cheek slowly.

"Hi…" My voice cracked as my vision blurred with tears. Although her hair was straighter and her eyes were a different shade, I was looking at Amara's twin.

She couldn't be more than two years old.

A small smile spread across her lips as she looked at me. "Auntie."

Nodding, I was so shocked she knew I was her auntie. But she turned abruptly and started running to the dark corner of the space. "Wait!" I called out as her hair flew behind her. Pushing myself off of the ground, I followed behind her. My lips parted as I saw a small hallway tucked away.

"Auntie!" she called out.

"I'm coming," I replied, picking up my pace.

But it wasn't me she was referring to as auntie. My eyes widened in shock as I walked in what resembled a small bedroom. There were two small cots, a few straggling blocks, and a few boxes of snacks.

But it wasn't the makeshift house that startled me; no, it was the frail woman in the corner racing toward the little girl.

"Stay away from her. Don't hurt her. Please!" she cried while clutching the frightened little girl.

Shaking my head, I put my hands up. "No, no. I'm not here to hurt you or her. I'm… I'm trying to help you escape," I said, my voice as low as possible.

"No, this is our home. It's dangerous out there." The woman tugged the little girl back into a shadowed corner.

Stepping forward, I looked at the little girl. "Is this your daughter?" I already knew she wasn't. The woman looked familiar, but I couldn't piece together how so.

"Yes. She's mine." She tilted her head and crossed her arms over the little girl's chest.

Nodding, I knew the woman was protecting the little girl. There was no way they were related. "Auntie!" the little girl chirped, but the woman slapped her hand across her mouth.

"I'm married to Raj." I swallowed and cradled my belly.

The woman's eyes widened. "He remarried?"

"You knew my sister, Amara?" I whispered and grew closer to the woman.

She began to cry. "No. But she's..." Looking down at the little girl, she pushed her toward me.

"She's yours. Save her. You have to save her. You know her birthday is soon. He's going to do it again and again. Her name is Shakti."

"Do what?" I trembled as I lifted the little girl into my arms. *Shakti.* It meant strength in Hindi. Amara knew this child had to be strong in order to survive. And she would survive.

"Sacrifice little girls to Dakini. The cemetery... he tries to sacrifice the dead, but it isn't enough. He said he'd have to try her next. Amara was his third wife. He's already sacrificed his other daughters from his previous wives.

My body shook as bile tickled my throat. No. This can't be happening. I couldn't breathe. He was truly a monster. He murdered his own daughters? Multiple wives?

She swallowed before she leaned, squinting. "Do you have to eat the mixture, too?"

My lips opened as my heart raced.

Blowing out a breath of air, I looked at the woman with confusion clearly plastered on my face. "What mixture?" I stammered.

Her body shook as she brushed her hands up and

down her arms. "You do. He makes meat out of the bodies before burying the rest of them."

I folded over, gripping my abdomen as stomach acid rose into my throat. "No, no…" Tears streamed down my face as I thought about what the hash-brown mixture was really composed of.

It… I… I ate another human being?

Vomit purged from my body violently as the little girl screeched and hid behind the woman.

My head was light, and the woman kept talking as if she hadn't just told me something that made me want to die.

"Is my mother dead? Is Mami dead?" She wiped under her eyes.

"I don't know who your mother is. I don't know who you are…" I gasped with my hands clutched around my throat.

"I'm Raj's younger sister."

CHAPTER
THIRTY-NINE

RAJ

"DON'T JUST STAND THERE! Help me!" my father screamed at me as I stared at my mother laying in a pool of blood.

She looked beautiful… more beautiful than she had ever looked. Tipping my head down, I smiled.

"You're just like me, my son. You feel the joy inside when a woman is where she belongs."

Lifting my mother's hands into mine, I dragged her body out of the room as my father quickly grabbed her legs.

A baby began crying in the background, which made my father wince. "What are we going to do with her?" I asked calmly, glancing at the baby.

"We will kill her tomorrow after we burn your mother."

Nodding, I knew better than to disagree with my

father. My mother gave birth to a daughter that my father was convinced would curse our family. He'd spend hours upon hours reading old Indian literature. How sons were the only way we could keep the family from being cursed or burdened. How women would be nothing more than a burden. Somewhere deep down inside, I think I always knew he'd kill my mother. He told me that women were meant to birth children, raise them, cook, and clean and then… there was nothing more than that. Being subservient to our families.

I suppose when you're told something your entire life, it's all you know. It becomes the truth. So, I believed him. I grew to resent women. I'd see the ones in town flaunting themselves in short dresses and tall heels while draping themselves over men.

Whores.

I knew I'd have to marry a good, traditional woman who'd obey me and give me a son.

———

I was the one who lit the match over the makeshift pyre that my father lovingly created for his bride. We stood there with the waves crashing and the full moon shining brightly. I tossed the match onto the body of the woman who gave me life. The woman who, for the most part, was kind and loving.

But love didn't mean anything. My father and I went back to the cliffside estate we purchased as soon as we moved from India when I was two years old. It was up for auction because of the decades of neglect.

As soon as we walked inside, I could hear her shrill cries. My father slapped his hands over his ears.

I walked over to the baby wrapped in a stained yellow blanket, my sister. My baby sister, yet I felt no emotion toward her. I wondered what was going through that little brain of hers? Could she sense the danger that was right in front of her or how her mother was now burning into ashes right outside the window that provided her with fresh air tinged with death?

My father came into the room carrying a garbage bag. "Move, Raj," he barked at me as he caught air in the bag before bending down to my sister. He was going to suffocate her. But just has he began pulling the bag over her head, his fingers began bending with a crack following each movement. His eyes widened as his spine straightened and he dropped the bag.

"Papa?" I looked at him as he stumbled back. Suddenly, the lights began to flicker rapidly. Red streaked the whites of his eyes as his hands trembled and each bone snapped. "Papa!" I screamed and tried to help him, but as soon as I grew closer to him, I could hear her voice.

My mother's voice reverberated loudly. "My baby!"

My father's eyes filled with fear as he looked at me pleadingly knowing we both heard her voice clear as day even though we'd only just watched her body burn to ashes. A cold blanket of air started to obstruct us as I turned to my baby sister.

"Kill her!" my father yelled as he slapped his hands around his neck and began to choke himself.

"Papa! Stop!" I tried to pry his hands off his neck to no avail. His tongue hung out of his mouth as he gasped and choked himself. I watched my father kill himself. I watched him choke himself to death.

But I knew he wasn't the one doing it.

"Ma," I whimpered as I walked backward into the wall. I didn't know what to do. My father fell to his knees and hissed, "That girl is cursed. Kill her!"

He collapsed, and I knew he was gone.

In the span of one evening, I'd become an orphan and a brother.

Looking at the small child, I lifted the bag my father left beside her. I had to finish what he had started. "My baby!" Her voiced echoed as I fell backward with a cold gust of air. Lying flat, my eyes shot open as I began sobbing.

Sharp nails dug into my skin as I screamed, "I won't do it! I won't kill her!"

Slamming my eyes shut, I screeched out in pain.

That was the first night of the rest of my life filled with a curse.

"What have you done, Raj?" My head turned slowly, and I saw our nanny, who we lovingly referred to as 'Mami'. She looked at my father, she could smell the fumes of my mother burning, and she saw the baby clutching a plastic bag.

I forced myself to stand and when I did, she ran away from me. She tried to run down the stairs, but I tripped her. I watched her tumble and her body broke against the curved stairwell before I grabbed the lamp sitting on the table and slowly walked down, allowing her to hear each step creak knowing her fate was sealed. But just as I slammed the steel lamp against her body and blood spewed, I heard a cry.

I didn't know how to take care of this baby. I needed a woman in this house to help.

Except, I had hurt Mami more than I realized.

I couldn't kill her; I needed to have someone else in this house with me. When the time came to marry, no one would trust a lone man with their daughter. Mami could be my family. A false pretense. I could be the caring, loving son caring for his now disabled mother.

No one would know I caused her to become this way.

Shaking my head, I had made a brilliant plan.

· · ·

But sins cut deeper than we can see. I didn't think what I had done or what my father had done was erroneous. Mami was mostly inadequate, but I'd leave the child in the bed with her so Mami could feed and change her. Luckily, she'd only become paralyzed from the waist down. Once the child grew up, I knew I risked her speaking and running away. But every single time I tried to end her life, I could hear my mother's sharp voice. The house would shake, the lights would flicker, and my hands would find their way to my own neck.

I could see the way my father painfully ended his life. But he hadn't done it alone—my mother had killed him. I knew it was her. She was haunting us. She wanted something from me.

Footprints would appear against the floor. The stove would catch fire. I'd wake up with scratches and blood seeping out of my flesh. I lost hope and feared waking up every single day, wondering if it'd be my last. The estate grew even drearier. I had grown tired of Mami's groans and somewhat caring for her. One day, I was in her room, staring at her and wondering if I should just suffocate her—perhaps strangle her with my bare hands? But just as I leaned down, her eyes shot open and her voice altered. It was deep, raspy, and terrifying.

"Dakini!" she screeched, looking behind my shoul-der. I felt frozen as my breathing became sparse. It was as if two icy-cold hands were wrapped around my throat, depleting my oxygen.

Dropping to my knees, I knew I didn't want to die. I wanted to carry my father's beautiful legacy. "No, please!" I begged.

Mami kept chanting 'Dakini' over and over again, her voice heavy and hoarse, until I made a deal with the devil.

"I'll do anything. Please! I'll do anything," I called out to no one.

The grip around my neck loosened and I sucked in a breath of air.

Slapping my palms against the ground, a tear fell from my eye. "Who is Dakini?" I asked, looking at Mami.

A smile crept across her face as she laughed wickedly. "I am Dakini."

Jumping to my feet, I ran out of her room, slamming the door behind me.

What had my father and I done?

"WE'VE GOT TO LEAVE." I pleaded with Raj's sister, Shanti. She hesitated as she walked in circles.

"Raj said that Dakini is out there." She pointed to the small trap door. Reaching out she brushed her hand against mine.

"You're so cold." She whispered.

I was becoming frustrated, knowing time was running out. Raj would soon wake and know I wasn't in bed.

Shanti lifted the little girl into her arms and backed away. "You just go. Please. We are fine," Shanti pleaded as I walked closer.

"My papa killed my ma. She became Dakini. Dakini comes to haunt and wreck the family that hurt her. My brother is cursed now until he offers her a sacrificial son."

My body was shaking with rage. I was running out of time. This woman must have been here for her entire life, convinced she'd die if she left. I had to get her out. I had to take this little girl away. This was my sister's daughter. I had to save her.

"Shanti, give me the little girl. Give her to me now. I promise you, no one is out there to hurt you." The little girl began kicking and wriggling out of Shanti's frail arms.

"No!" she screamed as the little girl bit her arm. Shanti released her and cried out in pain. I opened my arms wide as the little girl ran to me.

Lifting her up, I turned away as Shanti screamed behind us, "No!" But she didn't come closer. I knew her fear of the outside and unknown was greater than the love she had for this little girl.

I made my way to the ladder, sliding the little girl to my back. "Hold on!" As soon as I pushed the small door upward, we climbed out. A small gasp left the little girl. It was raining hard as my feet sloshed through the mud. Looking up at the estate, I could see a light turn on upstairs.

Raj was awake.

Thankfully, Raj left the backup keys to the hearse in the glovebox—he knew I'd never attempt to drive it. I didn't have a license and I'd never driven before, but I always studied him driving whenever we sat in it together. Picking up my pace, I could hear Shanti scream from below. She was too terrified to leave. Guilt trickled inside, but I had to save Amara's daughter. I had to save myself.

"Amara!" Raj raced toward the hearse. Clutching the little girl's legs, I moved faster; I was almost there. He was too far to make it to us.

"Amara! Stop!" he yelled.

"I'm Gia!" I cried as I opened the car door, flung the little girl in, and then slid inside. I slammed the doors and locked them as he grew closer. My hands shook wildly as I opened the glovebox and tugged the keys out. He wasn't wrong. I could feel something or someone inside of me using me to help

"Amara! My love, stop! You've come back to me even though I hurt you! You are back. I can't lose you again." Completely soaked from the rain, he slammed his fists against the window.

Jamming the key into the ignition, I turned it and pressed my foot against the gas. The tires grated against the gravel as Raj ran beside us until I sped up and left him behind. Glancing in the rearview, I could see him there, hunched over, knowing he had finally lost. The Rao family had lost.

I gripped the steering wheel and tried to remember my way back into the city as the little girl next to me started to sob.

"Mommy?" She looked at me.

Glancing at her as I drove, I shook my head. "No, no… I'm your auntie," I whimpered. "Your mommy was my sister." I smiled sadly.

It was finally over.

Adrenaline coursed through me as I passed through the dense wilderness that separated us from the city and life.

"Is your name really Shakti?" I asked her as I padded my thumbs against the worn steering wheel.

"Big box?" She was perched upright, looking in the back.

I looked back and realized a coffin was there. Swallowing the lump in my throat, I waved the little girl to sit back down.

"Nothing. It's nothing. Tell me your name."

"Kaia!" she chirped excitedly.

A dreaded feeling filled my abdomen. I kept driving silently until the estate was long gone, and I knew miles were put between us. I pulled over into the first parking lot attached to multiple shops, which was completely empty beyond a few lampposts. Swallowing the lump in my throat, I looked at the lights.

They began flickering, strobing rapidly. "Stay here." I looked at the little girl, who resembled me in many ways beyond those bright blue eyes.

Sliding out of the car, the rain slammed against my

body as puddles pooled around my bare feet. Walking to the back of the hearse, I opened the door and climbed into the back. My heart slowed as I traced my fingers across the cold steel. Digging my nails into the crevices and pulling the top of the long silver box, I gasped as soon as I saw her face.

"No." I shook my head as tears instantly filled my eyes and I looked at her body. She looked… *peaceful.* Her beautiful, once shiny black hair was tousled over her frail shoulders. Her once bright pink lips were now shriveled and pale. Her beautiful eyes were sealed shut. I brushed my fingers across the butterfly wing pendant that matched the one around my own neck. She had been here, right here, all along. The bruises all across her neck had my heart shatter.

Dropping my head, I cried harder and covered my mouth with my hands as my saliva and tears blended together. It was closure. The closure I thought I so desperately needed. Wanted. Had to have.

"Kaia is here!" the little girl sang from the front.

"Don't turn around, baby. Don't turn around." I forced through my sobs.

Blinking repeatedly, I slid the heavy lid back on the coffin and slammed the door shut. Wiping my nose with my arm, I couldn't believe this was it. This was the end. Walking through the rain, I felt invisible. The rain slanted harder, and I watched the drops fall to the ground, yet I didn't feel them.

Walking back around, my heart felt heavier than ever as I caught a glimpse of my reflection.

My breathing hitched.

Amara. I saw my reflection and it was hers. A moment later, I collapsed. Everything went black.

***

AMARA

Police sirens roared in the parking lot as Kai cradled the little girl in his arms and kissed the top of her head. A blanket of peace wrapped around me. I always felt cold but, in this moment, warmth comforted me as I saw the two true loves of my life. My daughter was reunited with her father. My daughter was finally safe. I had guided Kai to her. I had protected her.

Kai opened the door and held little Kaia in his arms. She was beautiful; she was the perfect mix of him and I. He never even knew she existed until I tried to lead him to her. He was the only person who could save her.

There was so much noise. Shouting, yelling, guns pulled out, and Kai screaming back at his innocence as he held our daughter in his arms. He was crouched down by Gia as paramedics lifted her up.

Some of the officers opened the back of the hearse as I stepped back and watched them pull the steel coffin out.

Flinging the top off, Kai began sobbing as the officers' faces grew grim while covering Kaia's eyes.

"It's her. That bastard killed her and had my daughter, our daughter… hostage in the bunker. There's another woman there. Raj Rao's sister," Kai spewed out.

"Sir, can you please tell us her name." An officer pointed to the coffin as I looked down into it once more.

"Amara." We both said at the same time. They couldn't see me. They couldn't hear me. I was looking down at myself, a woman with so many aspirations and dreams. A woman who was so excited to become a mother. A woman whose fate had been made and sealed for her.

Closing my eyes, a tear trickled down my cheek. I thought back to when I arrived in America with my handsome husband. His deep brown eyes and sun-kissed tan skin made my heart beat faster. I thought of how proud ma and papa were sending their daughter to America with an Indian-American doctor. I remember dreaming of what our future would hold with laughter and love. But then, Raj showed me his erratic side. The side where he would become possessed by something or someone.

The way his eyes would bulge and he'd drop to his knees chanting things that made no sense. I'd walk through the dusty, dark estate and hear the fingernails dragging across the walls or the distant screams and cries. But, as a duty to my parents I stayed. I knew my sister would never get married if I fled back home. I knew I couldn't risk Raj taking away financial assistance to my parents and their barely surviving farm. Death would be better than disappointing my parents. And so it came for me, in the form of my violent husband's hands.

Raj was angry that I had given birth to a daughter. He hated how happy I was brushing my finger against her plump cheek. So he killed me. He wrapped his hands around my neck as I sang to my baby girl who laid in bed beside us. He straddled my body and watched the soothing words and life leave my weak, postpartum body. A sinister smile curved on his face as he began singing the song for me.

My daughter cried and I pleaded through gasps of air. I clawed at his hands but there was nothing left in my body. He was in control. He always was.

The cries of our daughter pierced into me and what he didn't know was that Dakini, the spirit he was scared of was any woman who was murdered by her family and forced to leave behind her own child. Dakini always wins...*eventually.*

I became this Dakini, this powerful entity to help Kai find our daughter and to begin my revenge on Raj. I drove him into insanity through Gia.

"You have to catch Raj. He's a monster!" Kai shouted as he fought through tears looking down at my body. I walked closer to him. He was the love of my life. The kind of man that I didn't even dare to dream of. Wrapping my arms around him, I said goodbye.

Everything was going to be okay now. I couldn't save myself, but I saved her. Glancing at my beautiful little girl and the man I loved, I knew she'd break the cycle. She would make sure to live enough for the both of us. I just didn't think I could let her go...yet. I didn't think I could let him go either.

I watched Kai climb into the ambulance with worry in his eyes for Gia. He loved her...

A tear rolled down my cheek.

Betrayal.

FORTY-ONE

KAI

TIME HAD COME AND GONE. If someone would have told me that a few years ago, a beautiful raven-haired woman with gorgeous olive skin and almond-shaped eyes that were filled with something I'd never seen before would come into my restaurant with her husband and change my life forever, I'd have laughed.

But that's what happened. Amara was unlike any woman I'd ever met. Raj, her husband, would bring her to my restaurant once a week. I could tell how uncomfortable she was with him. I could see her pleading with those beautiful brown eyes to help her get out of the marriage she was forced into. Everything changed the day she slid me a note she'd scribbled out on a cocktail napkin while in the restroom.

Please help me.

So, I did. I drove out to the Rao Estate—the one that so many hushed ghost stories were about. I stood outside on the agreed day. I watched her tip-toe out of the house that I could feel a dark presence from when I flashed my car lights.

The moment her eyes caught mine, she smiled. But it wasn't just any smile; it was a smile full of hope and relief. We got into my car and drove in silence. It wasn't until we got into my penthouse that she threw her bruised arms around my neck and clutched me to her.

"You saved my life."

Four words that would forever haunt me. Because ultimately, I hadn't.

Raj hunted her down. It took him five months to find her, but it took me one month to fall in love with her and four months until she became pregnant. I didn't know. He dragged her home and threatened her with ruining her family's life in India. I couldn't understand the cultural disparities. But Amara had told me her little sister, Gia, would never get married or be respected if Raj told her village that she ran away with another man.

I tried to see her, but he wouldn't let me. I called the police, but they told me we were at fault—an extramarital affair. I was in the wrong, and there wasn't anything I could do.

I finally went back to the Rao Estate. I slammed my fist against the door and saw him. Raj looked like he hadn't seen sunlight in ages. His beard was grown out, the bags under his eyes sunken. He was muttering something to himself.

"Raj, where is Amara? Please, I just need to see if she's okay."

A sinister smile grew across his face. "She took the baby and left me to go back home to India. If you come back here, I'll chop you up and eat your body." He slammed the door, and I could hear him laughing through the thick wood.

Stumbling back, I immediately called the police. They told me to stop acting like some lovesick third wheel, told me to stay out of another marriage. Amara had a baby and there was a likelihood that child was mine. I felt her pleading with me every single day to get to her. I knew she was dead. There was no way he let her live.

So, I watched Raj from afar for weeks. I watched him go into the bunker with plates covered in tinfoil. I'd watch him come up with bags. I knew someone was living down there. I knew if I got the police involved, they'd wave me off.

Even if I had gone insane, I knew I had to be sure.

So, I took my tools to the hidden bunker door in the middle of a rainy night. I had to walk from the closest shopping strip, leaving my truck behind because I knew Raj would hear it puttering down the winding gravel. I knew I had to drive his hearse and escape with whoever he had held down there. Part of me, most of me, thought it was Amara. I had hoped it was her…

But it wasn't.

Even though she was with me all along, it wasn't the same. It'd never be the same. And I'd forever carry the guilt that I didn't save her. I could have saved her. I'm no hero.

———

Present Day
   Kai

"She's perfect." Gia wiped away her tears.

"I know," I whispered back. Guilt coursed through me knowing Gia had miscarried after collapsing in the parking lot and seeing Amara's body. At the hospital, the doctors stumbled back seeing Gia. Her skin was pale and lifeless. Her lips were shriveled. She looked dead and for a moment they did lose her.

Unfortunately that moment meant losing her child forever.

"I'll always be there for you, my little butterfly." Gia brushed her nose against my daughter's, who was now wearing the necklace her mother once wore.

I walked alongside Gia and Kaia outside. The skies were bright blue with the sun shining brightly for the first time in a long time. It was oddly beautiful considering we were walking through a cemetery.

"I would have done the cremation per Indian culture if…"

Gia looked up at me with the same eyes her sister captivated me with. "Kai, it's okay. Amara loved you, and I know she'd have wanted to be laid to rest the way you thought was best."

Kaia was wearing a black, frilly dress and tugging at Gia's hair.

Standing in front of the tombstone, I thought of everything that could have been. What would have been. What if I had left the city with her and saved her? What if I fought harder? What if…

But looking at Gia, I realized we all have 'what-if's' circulating through our minds. What if Amara was still here? Gia kept calling this spirit Dakini but I felt like it was my Amara all along. Amara could never become evil and that's what Dakini was the evil spirit that came from a woman who was murdered by the man she loved.

"I'm sorry I couldn't save you this time," Gia whimpered.

Looking at me, her eyes filled with tears. "When we were kids, I saved Amara from falling into a well. But now, I'm wondering if I killed her that day. If I had let her fall, she would have never gone through any of this." Gia choked out.

Tears rolled down my cheeks as I opened my arms for my daughter. "Then we wouldn't have her. So, thank you for saving the woman I loved and the mother of… the greatest gift in my life." I looked at the tombstone in front of me and handed Kaia a white rose to lay on her mother's grave.

Gia walked away, giving us a moment as a family of three.

"You saved her." I could hear Amara's soothing voice clear as day and smell the jasmine. Looking down at my arm, I felt something loop around it— something warm and familiar. A small gust of wind lifted around Kaia and I, moving the thick black hair away from her eyes.

"You can rest now. I've got our daughter. You can rest now," I cried as the warmth began to leave me… as Amara permanently left me.

But looking down at our daughter, I knew she'd

live on, and I'd make sure this little girl had every opportunity, every right, and every bit of support. I knew this little girl would make her mother proud. A small yellow butterfly fluttered around us. She was finally free. She didn't have to be trapped as Dakini anymore.

KAI HAD ASKED me if I wanted to stay with him and help with Kaia. My mother didn't care to hear about her granddaughter; I think she preferred to live in a state of ignorance. My father cried and said he'd come visit after learning I had lost my own baby. Kai offered to pay for flights, but I knew they'd never come. My mother called my sister a whore for sleeping with another man while she was married. She failed to hear the fact that her darling son-in-law was a psychopath currently in hiding somewhere. He had witnessed his father commit heinous crimes, and he had become the monster his father already was.

But that didn't give him the right to hurt my sister. To keep his own little sister locked up in a bunker because his father said women were burdens. It didn't give him the right to keep a baby girl down there. It didn't give him the right to ruin my life. He called me Amara and partly, he wasn't wrong. I think she was using my body in many ways to drive him insane and drive me to Kaia. There was always something cold and heavy inside of me while living in the Rao estate.

Raj's little sister was now in a psychiatric facility. She'd never seen sunlight and she truly believed that Dakini would kill her. Curiosity got the best of me, and I continued to research the Indian folklore about Dakini.

Perhaps it was true. Perhaps, all this time, Raj's mother had become this deranged, heartbroken spirit out for revenge and my sister had to become that too.

After all, Dakini was a tormented spirt that was usually a woman who died during childbirth, pregnancy, or simply a mother dying and knowing her child was left behind. A mother who loved her child so much that she couldn't bear to be without them. Raj had killed my sister after he saw how much the child meant to her. He wanted to kill Kaia, but I'm absolutely sure Raj was haunted and tormented by his mother and my sister.

His mother kept Raj's sister alive, and my sister kept Kaia alive. The Rao family had a century-old history of slaying the wives who birthed girls. They were obsessed with the idea that a daughter would curse the family.

Shanti, Raj's sister, had left detailed journals for the police to read through of her interactions with Raj, and briefly, her father.

According to her doctors, she was pleading to see Kaia. She thought of Kaia as her own daughter. She was obsessively sketching drawing after drawing of Kaia's face. I didn't think much of it, considering she was in a psychiatric facility with maximum security.

"Thanks for taking such good care of Kaia, Gia." Kai smiled at me as he diced vegetables. He'd worked all day in the restaurant, and then came home to cook delicious meals for the three of us. In exchange for taking care of my niece, whom I loved like my own child, Kai was paying for me to get my college education. I had my own bedroom, and Kai always asked me for my thoughts, opinions, and goals.

There were some moments that felt more than the original friendship that had blossomed from an otherwise dark circumstance, but guilt panged me. The way our fingers would brush against one another's as I handed Kaia over to him. Or the way we'd laugh over the things parents did when their child did something funny or silly.

"Try this, and tell me if you think it belongs on the

menu, please?" Kai handed me a fork with pasta twirled into a creamy white sauce.

Opening my mouth, I leaned in as he smiled and fed me.

"Mmm…." I moaned as I chewed the delicious pasta. "Absolutely, yes. Chef's kiss." I teased.

Kai leaned in to wipe the lingering sauce away from my lips before growing closer and pressing his mouth against mine.

Closing my eyes, I held my breath as Kaia giggled in the background. "Now that's a chef's kiss." He smirked as he pulled away but pressed his forehead against mine.

Suddenly, the lights began to flicker and the bowl of pasta slammed to the ground.

My heart began racing as I stood and looked up at the light and then back to Kai.

"Amara…" I whispered. Kai wrapped his arms around me and just as he did that the lights went out completely.

"Ah!" He cried out. Rushing away from him, I grabbed the flashlight and shined it over him. He was holding his arms as we both looked at the deep, bloody scratches all over them.

"It's not her. She'd never do this…" Kai's eyes watered as he looked back at me. The lights turned back on.

I sighed. Kai didn't think it was my sister but I knew better. It was Dakini the evil version of my once sweet sister.

Kai turned away to wash his arms.

"We can't do this…Kai." I hugged myself.

"She's gone. And I think she'd want us to be happy. Not just for her, or ourselves, but for Kaia, too."

Kai turned and slid a plate over to me as he held a towel against his arms.

"Explain that." I pointed to his wounds as the blood seeped through the white dish towel.

"I'm not going anywhere, Gia. I'll wait for you, and even if you want nothing more than… well, this, then that's fine, too. I feel complete peace with you and Kaia. I could want nothing more." He pulled out a cross and held it up. "I'm going to ask the priest to come over, tonight. I can't let this…whatever it is torment us."

I knew a priest couldn't rid of what this was. This was dark magic, this was something so far past religion and prayer. This was evil from pain and revenge.

Looking to Kai, I reached my hand out and opened my palm. "Okay." I smiled and exhaled not letting him see the fear inside of me.

"Gia, we can just… be. Be together. Be each other's someone. And yes, one day, I would love nothing more than to build a family and life together with marriage, but I know that's not what you want right now. I think we have some other issues we need to handle." He lifted his arm up.

"I don't think that will ever be handled." I spun the pasta around my fork and fought back the tears.

OPENING MY EYES SLOWLY, I watched the curtains dance slowly with the cool breeze rippling through.

"Save her," her voice brushed against my ear.

Blinking, I thought I was dreaming but her voice grew clearer. "Save her, Gigi." I could hear the desperation in her tone. Sitting up, I looked around. I didn't remember opening the window. Rubbing my eyes, I padded against the cold wood floor until I felt my fuzzy slippers.

Yawning, I opened my door and ran straight into Kai.

His eyes broadened as he looked at me with his forehead crinkled.

"You heard her, too, didn't you?" he whispered

loudly. Nodding, we both looked down the hall to Kaia's room.

"Kaia!" he screamed and sprinted toward her room as I followed close behind him.

As soon as he opened the door, he yelled, "Call 9-1-1, Gia!" But I didn't. I stood behind him as we watched the young woman sitting in Kaia's rocking chair, cradling her and singing the classic Hindi nursery song. Kaia was sucking her thumb and staring at the woman with adoration in her eyes.

"Listen… I need you to give my daughter to me now." Kai started to approach them, but I grabbed his arm from behind.

"The gun," my voice shook as I pointed at the shiny weapon resting next to the woman. She had a white nightgown on with her black hair hanging over her face.

She didn't look at us. She was brushing the hair from Kaia's face and kissed her head.

"Please, please just leave. We won't do anything if you just give us our daughter back," Kai begged her. I took a few steps backward into the hall and tip-toed back to my room. Getting my phone, I dialed the police, whispering our information. Though only a mere two minutes had passed, it felt like time had frozen as fear radiated through my body.

"You're just as beautiful as she was." A sharp voice behind me had my spine straightening and my hands freezing as I laid the phone back onto my nightstand.

Turning slowly, I saw Kai holding Kaia, looking at me with dread as the woman held a gun aimed right at me.

"Take care of our baby. She's... our baby." Tears streamed down her face as she moved backward out of the room. Kai pressed his back against the wall, covering Kaia as I stood there, paralyzed in panic but realization overtaking me.

It was Shanti. Raj's sister. She loved Kaia and raised her since she was a baby. She felt distraught without her. My heart was racing as sirens wailed outside our window, and I worried she'd fire the gun.

But she didn't; instead a small, eerie smile curved on her face as she walked backward into the darkness.

"I'm going to go after her!" Kai said as he directed Kaia to me.

"No! I can't lose you, too!" I raced over to him and put my arms out. "She has a gun. The police are here." I shut and locked the door quickly and tugged him to the corner Kaia was in. Within minutes, I could hear our front door being knocked down and officers yelling out. The three of us huddled together as Kai's strong arms held us protectively.

———

"Hello?" the officers called out, opening each door before ours.

"We're in here!" Kai jumped up and went to them with his arms up. Clutching Kaia to me, I looked down at her. She had no fear. She almost looked happy?

"Are you okay, baby?" I whispered into her hair as she sucked her thumb.

"Auntie!" she chirped. "Yea, it was, wasn't it?" I blew out a breath of air into her soft hair. Kaia never called me auntie, only Shanti. She called me Gigi… just like her mother once did when we were kids.

"Gia? Will you please come out? The officers need to speak with us." Gripping Kaia tightly to my chest, I walked outside cautiously.

A detective was waiting. "Hi ladies. Are you both doing okay?" he asked as he chewed the back of the ballpoint pen and flipped opened his notepad. The scent of cigarettes and coffee wafted off of him.

Nodding, I sank down next to Kai, who had his face in his palms.

"Gia, I just spoke to Kai about what you both saw… well, experienced tonight," the detective slowly said.

Kai looked up at me and put his arm around my shoulders as the detective spoke.

"Kai tells me that you both saw Shanti Rao. Raj Rao's sister?"

"Auntie!" Kaia giggled. The detective looked at her with the creases on his forehead and near his eyes deepening.

"It seems…" He paused as I parted my lips.

"What is it?" I looked at Kai.

"She…" Kai covered Kaia's ears before whispering to me, "She died a month ago, Gia."

My entire body went cold.

"No." I shook my head and licked my lips before turning back to the detective and handing Kaia back to her father.

"We saw her. Kaia saw her." I brushed my hand over my mouth.

"It's happening again." I turned to Kai. "The Rao family. The women all… They become tormented spirits. They never let go." Falling back into the couch, the lights began to flicker and the curtains began to dance wildly.

"It's going to be okay, Amara. I promise." Kai tilted my chin upward before leaning in to kiss me with a small, sad smile growing across his lips.

Pulling back, I looked at him.

"I'm Gia. Gia."

Shaking his head, he nodded with a sad smile. "I

know, I know…" Tugging me into his body, I looked over his shoulder and closed my eyes for a brief moment before opening them to a soft cry.

Kaia was in a woman's arms. A beautiful woman that looked like my sister surrounded by her gorgeous bridal outfit. But as she stood up her hair fell out from the neat bun and now the woman was staring back at me with anger as her black hair dripped over her shoulders. Her makeup was smeared, the whites of her eyes stood out with the smudged dark eyeliner and the maroon lipstick was hardly on her lips but covered her entire mouth and chin.

My heart pounded as she stood and carried Kaia. Everything was frozen around me. They both grew closer as I rested my chin on Kai's shoulder.

"You'll never be more than a shadow of me, my little butterfly. Raj needs to die. One way or another, he will die. Even if it's through you." She rasped as she brushed her nails across my cheek.

I held my breath as tears dribbled down my face. I knew nothing would ever be the same in my life. She was still here. She'd always still be here.

Later that night, I woke up and was rocking Kaia. It brought me so much warmth and peace. But it was fleeting as the door creaked open and I saw a shadow. One that made everything in the room feel cold.

I didn't want to believe that some evil spirit had

come from my sister and was haunting us. I wanted to believe she was watching us happily. But I could hear her crying in the corner of the room as if she were angry that I was here. What if she wanted to really… become me because I had to basically become her…

MONTHS HAD PASSED and the dust had settled just as it does with everything in life. Grief, pain, and even happiness comes in waves. Some more powerful and bigger than others. Some that make us feel like we are drowning. But I had learned to swim. Kai and I had found a new family dynamic of our own with Kaia. I felt happiness although I felt like a completely different person. My body didn't feel like my own, anymore. Perhaps living in my sister's shadow would mean never feeling the same.

The police never found Raj. He simply vanished into the night. Some think he killed himself. There was a note found along with his clothing by the cliff. It would make sense considering a man that was obsessed with death probably wanted to meet it on his own terms. My sister was brutally murdered and deprived of being the mother she always wanted to be. She was deprived of the life she always wanted, even though she was good. Truly good.

I tried my hardest to focus on living, but it was hard when a cloud of death seemingly followed me. Strange things were still happening in our home. Butterflies drawn in the steam of my shower, soft cries of a woman could be heard as I rocked my niece pretending to be her mother. We learned to live with it all. I knew it had to be my sister. She wasn't at peace. Was she resentful of me filling in her shoes? One night in particular, I felt cold hands around my neck as the air from my lungs left my body. I cried out and slapped at my neck but there was nothing physical there for me to remove. I just remember falling asleep and hoping she'd leave. Please just leave, sister.

But then a call came. Papa was dying and the doctor said he only had days left. Kai and I both agreed taking Kaia to India wasn't a good idea. Yet, I knew I had to go. I had to see Papa because if I didn't, I'd regret it.

***

I stood in front of the worn, red door. I could tell ma had tried to paint over it, but it only made it look worse. Lifting my hand, I went to knock at the door of the home that I had spent most of my life in. Childhood homes can be such a paradox. They are familiar yet foreign. Swiping away a straggling tear from under my eye, I exhaled.

The door opened and there she was. *My mother.*

The circles beneath her eyes were darker and deeper yet she didn't necessarily look sad.

"Gia," she sighed as if she were disappointed. Granted, she probably was. I'd never be her darling Amara. Begrudgingly, she wrapped her arms around me and gave my back a light pat.

"How is he?" I asked as I walked in. The light aroma of spices washed over me like a hug warmer than my mother's arms.

"Almost dead. This life brought him no peace. His daughters..." she clicked her tongue and shook her head.

Scoffing, I let out a dry laugh. "Yes, ma. Amara and I are the reason that he's dying. The daughters you never saw as anything more than a burden.

Anger filled my mother's eyes as she gritted her teeth. "You think you're better than me because you are American now?" She mocked.

Pausing in front of my father's door, I looked at her. "No, ma. I know I'm better than you. It's one thing to abide by culture and beliefs. I know so many of the arranged marriages truly do work out. I respect them and our beliefs. But what I don't respect is turning your back on your daughters when we both needed you." I opened the door slowly and saw him.

But it wasn't papa who had me gasping for air.

It was Raj.

My husband. My dead sister's husband.

"Ma!" I screamed and looked back at her. She didn't say anything beyond walking past me and going to him.

My heart was beating rapidly as I shook. "Ma…" tears rolled down my cheek as I watched her wrap her arms around Raj's shoulders.

He looked up at me with a small smile.

"The moment I married Amara, I became this family's son. And don't forget, you're still my wife, Gia. I actually stood by them unlike both of you. This is why having a son is valuable. This is why having a daughter is nothing more than a burden. I feel sorry that such a loving ma has to live with two whores as her daughters. This is why your papa is dead. I thought this entire time I was remarried to you…but I knew deep down inside my Amara was right there still." Raj fired at me as my mind felt fuzzy.

Everything started to blur.

"Papa…is dead?" I questioned while I choked on my words. Walking over to him, I sunk down beside his body and watched as his chest didn't rise and fall. There was an odor surrounding his body.

"How long?" My voice cracked as I looked up at my mother and the monster next to her.

"How long!" I screamed and stood.

Ma came around towards me and with one swift motion she slapped me.

"What are you doing, Gia?" She shouted at me as her spit splashed across my face.

I began sobbing as I clutched my cheek. "Ma…" I felt like I was a child. A scared child.

"I thought you at least loved Amara…if you loved her why would you have him here? He killed her, ma. He abused me. He tried to kill me. He had his own little sister and Amara's daughter as a prisoner. He held me as a prisoner." I looked back at my lifeless father. My mother stood between us.

"Leave, Gia. Go back to the man who won't even marry you because you're living there like you're his mistress. You are nothing more than a dishonor to this family. Amara means nothing to me. She broke her vows to her loyal husband and had an affair. She had a child with a man that wasn't her husband when all Raj wanted was a family. I will not listen to you disrespecting my son. You couldn't even carry his child to term." She seethed.

"Ma…" I stumbled back as my nose and eyes dripped while my hand brushed against my stomach.

She was protecting her precious son-in-law. She had made her choice.

"Raj will light the pyre fire and will stand by me as we burn your father's body. Don't come, Gia. Your father wouldn't want you there."

"No. He will not light the fire. That is my papa. That is my duty." I protested.

"Leave, Gia and never come back. We will set your father free tomorrow and I don't want you near us." Ma said coldly.

Nodding my head, I knew I had no fight left in my body. "Ma, I have nowhere to go. I'll have to book a flight. Please let me stay here tonight. I beg you." I sniffled.

Ma looked back at Raj as if it were his house and she needed his permission. "Ma, let her stay tonight. I'm here to protect you from her." His thick brows knitted together as he smiled at me.

"Okay, one night." She agreed.

Raj stood and towered over me, "I'll get you pregnant again, my love." Clutching my face between his palms, he leaned in and bit my lip until I tasted blood.

My mother laughed in the background as I cried.

CHAPTER
FORTY-FIVE

GIA

THE DRY, hot air made it hard to breathe as the old box fan did nothing beyond blowing suffocating dust into my lungs.

Ma was out at an aunty's house praying through the night for papa's soul. She left me with my sister's murderer and well, my husband. The same husband who had raped me, tried to kill me, and tore my life to shreds.

I didn't hear footsteps so I assumed he was asleep. Taking a deep breath, I tip-toed out of my room that was now nothing more than a storage space and looked out into the darkness. The moonlight shimmered through a window as I walked to my father's room.

Clutching my stomach, I went in and looked at him.

Brushing my fingers across his wrinkled face, I shook my head.

"I'm sorry papa. I'm so sorry you didn't have sons. But Amara and I tried to do everything right for you and ma. It would have never been enough. We would never be enough." I whimpered.

The lights suddenly flickered rapidly as I stepped back from papa. The curtain began to sway even though there was no breeze. Papa's mouth hung open as his head dropped to the side and I noticed something on his neck. They were clear finger-shaped marks lining his flesh.

Someone had strangled my father to death. Someone who knew my father would never let a man who murdered his daughter live in his home.

Raj killed my father and my mother let him. In Indian culture, lighting the fire of the pyre for a funeral is a form of honor.

A son gets preference and if there is no son, a male relative does.

My father was different. He went with tradition and what my mother wanted because that's all he ever knew. What I knew is that he'd want Amara and I to light the match to lead him to his next life.

Maybe we'd find each other there.

Leaning down, I planted a kiss on my father's head. I noticed something else. Pulling his hand out from the blanket completely, a few fingers were missing. My stomach tumbled.

I knew Raj was sick. The freezer found in his home filled with perfectly packed up freezer bags filled with human remains. Raj would claim to bury the unloved but the cemetery in his front yard was nothing more than a place to store bodies before he turned them into food for himself.

My breathing grew erratic. How did my mother not know what was happening in her own home? How could she allow this?

I walked backwards out of the room, before making my way to the kitchen.

My hands shook as I prayed I was wrong. But as I opened the small refrigerator, I gagged. The smell was there but worst of all, so were the containers with labels.

Raj. Written in my mother's handwriting. She was just as sick as him.

Slapping my hand over my mouth, I could feel the stomach acid rise in my throat. Reaching into the drawer, I knew what I had to do.

It was the only way.

Turning outside, I looked at the tiny house and walked around the back to the window of where Raj was sleeping soundly. My skin was crawling as I thought of him living in peace while he destroyed my entire family.

I grew up believing only a son could protect his family, only a son could honor them. Reaching for the gasoline that papa always used for his tractor, I began pouring it all around the home that created me.

The strong scent burned my nose as it sloshed against the ground. Ma would come home and see her house gone. She'd know I did it. But it wasn't just to destroy Raj. No, it was because I had to be the one to light the match for papa. Not him. This would be the only way my father would rest, this would be the only way for my sister to finally rest.

Once I was back around, I stood and knew I'd light the match and throw it next to the room where Raj was. He wouldn't have time to escape. This house was built of such flammable materials it would be fully engulfed before he could wake and think clearly.

My fingers shook as I pressed the match against the matchbox. "Do it, Gia." I whispered to myself.

I was terrified. I was about to kill someone. I was about to burn my father's body and the only home my family ever truly knew.

Where would ma go?

But just as my fingers grew weak, I felt something.

I felt someone. I could hear her bridal gown dragging against the dirt, I could hear her thick gold bangles jingle but I didn't turn around. Her hand wrapped around mine and a hushed voice trickled into my ear.

"It's time, little butterfly. It's time to put papa to rest but also…" Tears fell from my eyes and I knew that my sister was here. Part of me thought she hated me or was going to haunt me. But it wasn't true. She was trying to guide me here and help me end all of this.

Nodding my head, "it's time to let you rest, too, Amara. I don't want Dakini to ever come back." I choked out as we lit the match and I watched the small flame burn.

Turning, I watched my sister walk into our childhood home adorned in her gorgeous bridal dress and beautiful jewelry.

Just as the door slammed behind her, the flame began burning my thumb and finger. Throwing the match down, I stepped back and took a deep breath in.

There were shrieks. His and hers. In an Indian wedding, the husband and wife walk around a blazing fire together as they vow seven lives together. They walk around that fire promising love, trust and loyalty. Today, my sister didn't burn with her husband, she burned him with me.

He was shrieking in pain and she was crying out in relief.

We burned our father's body together, like the good sons do. But together, we were better than any son.

Neighbors ran out of their homes while some shouted for buckets of water.

I crossed my arms and stood there watching the spectacle. The aunty my mother was supposed to be with reached over and shook me.

"Where is your mother?" She screamed. My eyes widened.

"I thought she was with you?" I gasped. She shook her head and looked back to my burning home.

Through the flames, I could see my sister's face and a small smile tipping against her beautifully lined red lips. I felt my own lips turn into a smile.

Drawing a butterfly into the soot of the window just as it shattered, I knew.

She wanted an end and a beginning. An end for my mother who would never change and kept her murderer alive but also a beginning for her daughter.

Turning around, I began hugging myself and walking down the small, darkened dirt road. Looking down, my heart began to race as I was wearing a bridal gown. Touching my neck, I was wearing jewelry and my arms were covered in soot as my flesh felt burnt. *What was happening?* I could feel the air in my lungs feeling constricted as if someone was here trying to steal my life.

My neck cracked upward as I looked at the darkened sky and my body tensed. No one could hurt me. No one could take my life from me. My eyes widened as my mouth dropped open, "Amara, please no!" I screamed. But my body stiffened. The world spun around me and suddenly, stillness.

Smiling, I knew that I had won and anyone who got in my way would die. I threw my head back and let my once beautiful gown drag against the pavement as I laughed wildly into the darkness knowing no one could ever kill me or take what I deserved. A small yellow butterfly danced around me. *"Kai is mine. You can't have him. You had to die, my little butterfly…"* I smiled. He'd never know that I wasn't Gia but his true love was back to him.

THE TIMES NEWSPAPER

LOCAL WOMAN ARRESTED after beloved restaurant-owner Kai Matthews was found pinned to the wall with nails drilled into his palms. Customers were traumatized when they went inside to dine and saw the owner in that state with blood pooled at the floor beneath his dangling feet. His young daughter was sitting in it and authorities say she had drawn an image from her father's blood of a woman with long hair and a smile that police say sent chills up their spine.

Neighbors say they'd often hear a woman's voice speaking with Kai and the young daughter but never saw her.

One neighbor stated she even peeked over the fence and saw Mr. Matthews and his daughter laughing and looking in the same direction talking to someone but no one else was there.

Police are seeking any and all help from the community. The little girl was giggling as she was taken away and placed in protective custody with a psychological evaluation to follow. There was a message written on the wall next to Mr. Matthews body in what police say may be the victim's blood.

"Now we can be together forever."

Please reach out to our hotline if you have any information regarding this case.

"Come with me, my little butterfly." I whispered as I brushed the hair from Kaia's face and tucked it behind her ear. I looked around at the other children in the group home but no one could see me as I laced my fingers into hers and we walked out.

"Mommy's here now…" I whispered. "She'll never leave."

Thank you so much for reading The Arranged Marriage!

The Caged Girl is my next thriller novel and is the partner to The Favorite Girl.

Thank you so much for reading The Arranged Marriage. This is my only paranormal thriller which was written to celebrate my love for ghost stories and horror movies. I wanted to take a moment to explain the ending and the book a bit more since I know the cultural aspect of "Dakini" can be one that needs extra explanation.

I grew up hearing this folklore about women who are killed by their in-laws or husbands and then they come back as a Dakini, which is their spirit but an evil one. One that is angry and full of revenge. Unfortunately, Dakinis' thrive off of pain and feel wronged. They alter their spirit to be wicked. Here we see Amara's spirit guiding Kai and Gia throughout the book to find her daughter and eventually kill Raj. Once all of this is done we know Amara's spirit (Dakini) is not at peace knowing Gia and Kai are together living their own happily ever after.

So, at the end of the book we know Amara takes possession of Gia's body and goes back to Kai. However, the evil in her makes her eventually kill Kai because now they can be together forever in the after life but she wanted him to suffer first for ever loving Gia, hence the painful death.

I was the first person in my entire family not to have an arranged marriage so this book was highly requested by my mom and aunts who had plenty of stories on their own experiences. Some actually have had creepy paranormal encounters which I probably shouldn't had known about as a child but hey, now I write twisted thrillers so it worked out.

I hope that helps! Thank you for reading my spin on a ghost story!

ABOUT THE AUTHOR

Monica Arya is a Top 35 Amazon bestselling and award-winning author. She lives in Charlotte, North Carolina with her husband, two beautiful children and goldendoodle. Besides writing, Monica loves traveling, chocolate and sparkling water. Monica loves connecting with readers on social media. You can find her below on all platforms.

Facebook reader group : Monica Arya's Misfits for exclusive content and first look into new books.

ALSO BY MONICA ARYA

Thrillers

Girl in the Reflection

Shades of Her

The Next Mrs. Wimberly

Navy Lies

Don't Believe Him

The Favorite Girl

The Caged Girl

Romance

Saved by You

Misfit

When Love Breaks Us

ACKNOWLEDGMENTS

To my husband and children, Mila and Ari-thank you for being 'home' to me. And not a haunted home but one full of laughter and love. I love you all more than all the words can say. Above all being yours is the greatest gift in this world.

To the ones that are so special to me beyond the words - Paige, Joselin, Marcie, Marisha, Katie, Kori, Jackie, Allyson, Erin, Kealey, Gabby, Elise, Kelly, Amanda, Nikki and Sammie. I can't even begin to thank you wonderful humans for everything.

To my ARC team who have celebrated each book and ME to the point that I'm moved to tears. It is such an honor to have connected on this journey and each of you are so precious to me.

To my beloved readers-without you I wouldn't get to do what I love and I'm forever grateful for the time you take to read my books!